HONUS & ME

A BASEBALL CARD ADVENTURE

DAN GUTMAN

AN AVON CAMELOT BOOK

AVON BOOKS, INC.
1350 Avenue of the Americas
New York, New York 10019

Copyright © 1997 by Dan Gutman
Published by arrangement with the author
Library of Congress Catalog Card Number: 96-31439
ISBN: 0-380-78878-0
www.avonbooks.com

First Avon Camelot Printing: March 1998

CAMELOT TRADEMARK REG. U.S PAT. OFF AND IN OTHER COUNTRIES, MARCA REGISTRADA, HECHO EN U.S.A

Printed in the U.S.A.

OPM 10

For Ray Dimetrosky

Everything in this book is true,
except for the stuff I made up.

The following people were kind enough to help with this book: Dennis and Jeanne DeValeria, Bill Deane, Pat Kelly, Bill Burdick, and Milo Stewart of The National Baseball Hall of Fame, David Pietrusza and Bob Bluthardt of The Society of American Baseball Research, David Kelly of The Library of Congress, Gill Pietrzak of The Carnegie Library of Pittsburgh, Sally O'Leary of The Pittsburgh Pirates, Tom Mortenson of The Sporting News, Ted Taylor of Fleer Corp., Nina Wallace, Stephanie Siegel, The Haddonfield Public Library, Jeff Samoray, Jerry Cosover, Jack Kavanagh, Allen Barra, Liza Voges, Julie Alperen, Art Hittner, Philip Von Borries, Harold Berlin, Jon Kwartler, and David Plaut.

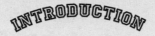

INTRODUCTION

THE FIRST TIME I TOUCHED A BASEBALL CARD, I FELT A strange tingling sensation all over my body.

It was sort of like the feeling you get when you touch your fingers lightly against a television screen when the set is on. Static electricity jumps off the glass and onto your skin, or something like that. I'll never forget it.

I must have been four or five the first time this happened, but ever since then I've felt that feeling whenever I touched certain baseball cards. It's kind of creepy.

I never got the tingling sensation from football cards or basketball cards. A plain old piece of cardboard wouldn't do it (believe me, I tried). Only baseball cards, and only *certain* baseball cards. Old cards worked best.

I never knew what was going on with these baseball cards, but I always thought there was something—oh, *magical*—about them. Then something happened to me that made it all clear. And that's what this story is about.

Joe Stoshack

PLAYING HARDBALL

1

"HEY! ELEPHANT EARS! WHEN YOU WALK DOWN THE street, Stoshack, you look like a taxicab with both doors open!"

The words burned in my ears, which *do* stick out a little from my head, I must admit.

I was at the plate. It was two outs in the sixth inning, and I was the last hope for the Yellow Jackets. We were aown by a run, and the bases were empty. Their pitcher was only eleven, but he'd already whiffed me twice.

That crack about my ears threw me off, just enough so that I tipped the ball instead of hitting it with the meat of my bat. That was strike two.

Behind me, I could hear some of the kids on my team already packing up their equipment to go home.

There wasn't much chance that I was going to smack one out of the park. I hadn't hit one out of the *infield* all season.

It's not that I'm not strong. My arms are really big, and people tell me my chest is broader than any other seventh grader they've seen. I'm short for a twelve-year-old and a little stocky.

I'm actually a pretty good ballplayer. But those insults really get to me. The last time up, I struck out when they said my legs looked like a pair of parentheses. You know—(). Bowlegged? I guess I'm kinda funny-looking. If I wasn't me, I'd probably be making fun of me, too.

Nobody likes to make the last out. I sure didn't want to strike out looking at the last pitch whiz past me. I was ready to swing at just about anything. The pitcher went into his windup again, and I stood ready at the plate. The pitch looked good, and I brought back my arms to take a rip at it.

"Hey Stoshack!" their shortstop shouted as the ball left the pitcher's hand, "Is that your nose or a doorknocker?" I'd never heard *that* one before. It threw off my timing. It felt like a good swing, but I hit nothing. As usual.

"*Steeerike threeeeeeeeeeeee!*" the ump yelled as the ball smacked into the catcher's mitt.

Again. My third strikeout of the game. Did I swing over it? Under it? Too early? Too late? I couldn't even tell. All I know is that I wanted to shrivel up and fade away. The other team hooted with glee. Even some of my teammates were snickering.

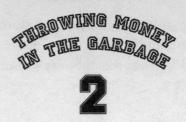

2

"JOEY, I'M HOME!" MOM SHOUTED AS THE SCREEN DOOR slammed behind her. "How was the game?"

"Lousy," I reported honestly. "I fanned three times and let a grounder go between my legs to let the winning run score."

Mom threw her arms around me and ran her fingers through my hair.

"You'll get 'em next time, slugger."

She flopped down in a chair. I could tell she was exhausted. Mom is on her feet most of the day. She works as a nurse in Hazelwood Hospital here in Louisville.

"So what did you make me for dinner?" she asked with a smile, "I'm beat."

"Oh, Mom, let's go out to eat tonight."

"Negative," she replied. "When you sign your big

6

league contract, you'll take me out on the town. 'Till then, we're on a tight budget."

"Fast food?" I suggested hopefully.

"Ugh!" she replied, holding her nose. "I'd rather starve."

I wouldn't say we were *poor,* but I sure wouldn't say we were rich either. We never had a lot of money, but things got really tough after my parents split up two years ago. My dad lived in Louisville too, in an apartment. He came over to visit from time to time.

Money was always a problem. When I was a little kid my folks used to argue a lot about it. Dad always seemed to have a tough time landing a job. When he found one, he never seemed to be able to hold on to it very long.

I've always thought that if only my parents had had more money, they wouldn't have split up. Mom said that was ridiculous. Money had nothing to do with it, she told me. Besides, she said, money doesn't make you happy.

But how would she know? She never had any.

I always wished I had a million dollars. At least I could see if she was right or not. Even a half a million would have been nice.

Until we win the lottery, I'd try to make a few dollars here and there doing odd jobs. Yard work. Raking leaves and stuff. The winter before, Kentucky got a lot more snow than usual, and I made a bunch of money shoveling people's sidewalks and driveways. I gave some of the money to my mom. The rest of it I spent on baseball cards.

Dad gave me his baseball-card collection and got me started collecting cards when I was seven. I may not have been a great hitter, but I knew more about cards than any kid around. I put together a complete set of guys who played shortstop. That was always my position.

Mom says buying baseball cards is like throwing money into a garbage can. But I figure a kid should be allowed to have one harmless vice. It's not like I drink or take drugs or anything.

And besides, my baseball cards actually *saved* us money. When I got holes in my sneakers, I would slip a card inside so I didn't need to buy a new pair right away. I always used lousy cards, of course. I wouldn't think of stepping on a card that was worth anything.

"I got you some work today, Joe," Mom said as we chowed down on leftovers.

"Oh, yeah? What?"

"Miss Young needs her attic cleaned out. She'll pay you five dollars. I told her you'd take it."

"Oh, *man!*"

Amanda Young is this really old lady who lives next door. I know she's way over one hundred, because my mom showed me an article from the paper that talked about Louisville's Century Club. She's pretty peppy for an old lady. Her skin is really wrinkly, though.

Miss Young never had any kids, and she was never married. I don't even think she has any relatives who are still alive. She's been living by herself in that dilapidated old house for as long as anybody can remember. She never comes outside. Her groceries are brought in.

My mom stops over to Miss Young's now and then to see if she's okay. I guess that's how I got this job.

It's not like I don't appreciate the work or anything. It's just that Amanda Young is kinda weird. I've run a few errands for her, and she starts talking to me about nothing and she goes on and on. I can't understand what she's saying half the time. I nod my head yes to be polite.

Sometimes, I must admit, I pretend my mom is calling so I can go home. Miss Young doesn't hear very well, so she can't tell I'm lying.

I've never seen Miss Young smile. She seems really sad, as if somebody did something terrible to her a long time ago and she never got over it.

I've heard kids say that Amanda Young is a witch, and that she murdered some kid once. Kids always make up stories like that. I think she's just a lonely old lady. I feel a little sorry for her.

Cleaning out Miss Young's attic isn't my idea of a fun afternoon, but five bucks is five bucks. Fleer is coming out with a new set of baseball cards next month, and I can use the money to buy a few packs.

I'm sure I would have felt differently about the job if I'd known what Miss Young had up in her attic.

A PIECE OF CARDBOARD

3

WE ONLY HAD A HALF DAY OF SCHOOL THE NEXT DAY, SO I thought it would be a good time to go over to Amanda Young's house. The shutters were hanging off the windows at an angle, and the place hadn't had a coat of paint in decades. You could tell home maintenance was not very important to the old lady.

Miss Young was in worse financial shape than we were. My mom said she could barely live off her Social Security checks.

After I rang the doorbell, I didn't hear a sound inside for a minute or two. I was afraid that maybe Miss Young was hurt or something, but then I heard her shuffling feet coming toward the door. She was really small, so when she opened the door a crack I could barely see her.

"Come in," she creaked. "Why Joseph Stoshack, you're getting to be *so* big!"

Inside, the house was like one of those historical houses some famous guy lived in and has been preserved just the way he left it when he died. It was filled with antiques, though I don't know if stuff is still called antique if somebody never stopped using it. The walls were covered with hats and dried flowers and old guns.

I couldn't imagine Miss Young firing a gun, but you never know.

"Pirates, eh?" she said, peering at my baseball cap. "Are you a Pittsburgh rooter?"

"No, I just like this baseball cap, Miss Young."

"I used to root for the Pirates when I was a girl," she said. "Well, one Pirate anyway." She stopped for a moment and let out a sigh before changing the subject. "We didn't have television back then, or even radio. But we used to *pore* over the newspaper. Did you know that the manager of the Pirates invented those flip-up sunglasses outfielders wear?"

"Really?"

Miss Young had never brought up baseball the other times we'd spoken. For the first time, she had my interest.

"That's right," she continued. "His name was Fred Clarke. He's a Hall of Famer, you know."

I had heard of Clarke, but I didn't know too much about him.

"And the baseball bat was invented right here in Louisville, Joseph. There was this fella named Pete Browning. He broke his bat one day, and a little boy took him home and carved Pete a new one on his daddy's lathe. His dad was a woodworker you see, who made wooden butter churns. Do you know what a butter churn is, Joseph? Oh, of course not. You're too young. Well, anyway, Pete took his new bat and got three hits the next day. Naturally, his teammates *all* wanted new bats. The woodworker stopped making butter churns and went into the bat business. And that's how the Louisville Slugger was born. Of course, that was before my time."

I couldn't imagine *anything* being before her time.

"I want to show you something, Joseph."

She put on a pair of old-lady glasses and opened a drawer in the bureau in her front hallway. After sifting through the junk in there for a minute, she pulled out a photo and held it under a lamp. It was an old-time baseball player. The image was fuzzy, but I could make out the word "Louisville" across the chest of his uniform.

The photo looked like it had originally been larger, but it was ripped in half. There was a white border at the top, bottom, and left side, but the right side had no border and the edge was jagged.

The picture had been taken in a garden. The ball-player was facing the camera and his left arm was extending out to the jagged edge, like he was holding hands with someone. It was impossible to tell who the other person was, because that half had been ripped off.

I looked up and saw there were tears in Miss Young's eyes.

"I was supposed to hold onto this half of the picture until we saw each other again," she said softly. "I waited and waited. But he never came back."

She handed me the picture abruptly. "Throw it away with the rest of the junk upstairs. It's worthless."

I'm a collector. I never throw *anything* away. Who knows? A ripped picture of an old-time ballplayer might be worth something to somebody. It certainly meant something to Miss Young a long time ago. As I stuffed the picture in my backpack, I wondered why it had made her so upset.

Miss Young led me upstairs and told me she wanted me to take everything out of the attic and put it on the street for the garbage men to take away. I figured she knew she wasn't going to live forever, and she wanted to clean up her affairs while she was still around.

As soon as I stepped up into the attic, I knew it had been a mistake to take the job. It was dark, filthy, and it looked like a junkyard. This was no five-dollar job, I thought to myself.

But a deal is a deal. I started picking through the trash and hauling it out to the street. The whole time I was thinking I should have gotten a paper route or some other real job.

Being a collector and all, I couldn't resist peeking into a few of Miss Young's old boxes to see what kind of stuff she had decided to hang on to all these years. But it was exactly what she said it was—worthless junk. Broken candlesticks. Old clothes. A set of encyclopedias. I chucked it all out.

After a couple of hours I had cleared the entire attic except for a few boxes. I was dog tired, and I picked up the next box without holding it from the bottom. The box had deteriorated with age, and the bottom ripped open in my arms. The contents spilled all over the floor. I was angry at myself for not being more careful.

I decided to take a short break before cleaning up the mess, so I lay down on the dusty wooden slats and stared at the rafters. In a few minutes I felt rested and rolled over on my side to look at the junk strewn across the floor.

It was papers, mostly. Nothing too interesting. Bank statements and tax returns from a long time ago. I started picking them up and putting them into a pile. When I picked up the stack, a single piece of cardboard fell out and fluttered to the floor.

This is what it looked like . . .

It didn't register at first. But when I picked up the card, I felt a strange tingling sensation.

I turned over the card and looked at the other side. I couldn't believe my eyes.

4

IT WAS A PICTURE OF A MAN'S FACE. I GASPED. INSTINCT-ively, I looked around to see if anybody was watching. Of course nobody was there.

The man in the picture was a young man, with short brown hair parted in the middle. He had a solemn expression on his face, with his head swiveled slightly so he was looking off to the left. His shirt collar was navy blue, and the shirt was muddy gray. It had four white buttons.

On the right side of his chest were the letters "PITTS" and on the left were the letters "BURG." There was no H.

The background of the card was burnt-orange. There was a thin white border on all four sides. Across the bottom border, centered in the middle, were these magic words . . .

WAGNER, PITTSBURG

My breath came in short bursts. I suddenly felt warm. My heart was racing. My *brain* was racing. The tingling sensation was all over me, and stronger than I had ever experienced it.

No doubt about it. I had just stumbled upon a T-206 Honus Wagner card—*the most valuable baseball card in the world.*

Every serious collector knows the legend behind the Wagner card. These early baseball cards were printed by tobacco companies and were included with their products. All the players agreed to be on the cards except for Honus Wagner, the star shortstop of the Pittsburgh Pirates.

Wagner was against cigarette smoking, and he didn't want his name or picture used to sell tobacco. He forced the American Tobacco Company to withdraw his card—but they had already started printing them. A small number of the cards reached the public before the card was discontinued.

That's why the Honus Wagner card is so valuable. Only about forty of them are known to exist in the whole world, most of them in bad condition.

I just found No. 41, and it was *mint*. Nobody had *touched* it in over eighty years.

I knew the piece of cardboard in my hand was worth thousands of dollars, but I didn't know exactly how *many* thousands. I remembered that a few years ago some famous athlete had bought one at an auction, but I couldn't recall who he was or how much he paid for it. It was a huge amount of money, that was for sure.

All my problems, I suddenly realized, were solved. Or so I thought.

I slipped the card in my backpack, being careful not to bend any of the corners or damage it in any way. A tiny nick in a card this rare might decrease its value by thousands of dollars.

Quickly, I gathered up the rest of the junk in the attic and hauled it out to the curb.

I had almost forgotten about Miss Young, but she called me over just as I was about to run home.

"Aren't you forgetting something, Joseph?"

She held out a five-dollar bill and shakily placed it in my palm. She grabbed my other hand and looked me in the eye.

"Thank you for helping out an old lady," she said seriously. "And because you did such a fine job, I want you to have *ten* dollars. I bet that's a lot of money to a boy your age."

Ten bucks? In my head I was thinking that I had a fortune in my backpack.

"Yeah, I could use ten dollars," I sputtered. "Thanks Miss Young."

"Buy something nice for yourself," she called out as I dashed away. "Money won't do *me* any good."

"I will," I called out as I left. "Believe me, I *will*."

Mom wouldn't be home from work for an hour or so. I grabbed my bike, hopped on, and started pedaling east on Chestnut Street past Sheppard Park and Founders Square.

As I cruised down the streets I was filled with an overwhelming feeling of joy. Happiness washed over my body. Nobody could touch me. Nobody could hurt me. Nobody could tell me what to do. It was a feeling I had never experienced before.

I didn't know if I should tell the whole world about my good fortune, or if maybe I shouldn't tell *anybody* in the world.

As I whizzed down the street, I felt like everyone was looking at me. I felt like everyone must somehow know what had happened to me. They knew what I had in my backpack. It was as if the news had instantly been picked up on CNN and broadcast around the globe.

Those feelings lasted about a minute, when a different feeling came over me. A bad feeling. The baseball card wasn't mine to take, really. It was Miss Young's card. If anybody deserved to get rich from it, it was *her*. She had been nice enough to pay me *double* for cleaning out her attic, and I had stolen her fortune.

Almost as quickly, my brain came up with reasons I shouldn't feel badly. Miss Young herself said that money wouldn't do her any good, so why *shouldn't* I keep the card? After all, *she* told me to throw the stuff away. If I hadn't found the card, *she* wouldn't have found it. It would have ended up buried in a landfill someplace, worth nothing to anyone.

Finder's keepers, right?

And besides, I thought, Miss Young isn't going to live much longer.

I felt bad, again, thinking that last thought.

I was feeling very mixed up. Deep inside I knew the right thing would be to give Miss Young back her baseball card.

But that didn't necessarily mean I was going to *do* the right thing.

"I'LL GIVE YOU $1,000 CASH RIGHT NOW."

5

BIRDIE'S HOME RUN HEAVEN WAS A COUPLE OF MILES EAST from my house, in River City Mall on Broadway in Louisville. I pulled into the parking lot and skidded my bike to a stop in front of the door. The neon lights behind the window spelled out "COMICS," "COLLECTIBLES," and "BASEBALL CARDS." Below was a sign that said, "BUY . . . SELL . . . SWAP."

"I need to speak with Birdie," I told the teenager working the counter.

"Birdie's busy," he said with a snotty tone in his voice. The teenager obviously thought he was hot stuff because he had a job in a baseball-card store.

"It's important," I shot back.

Ordinarily, I'm a pretty shy kid, but somehow having the Honus Wagner card in my backpack was giving me a surge of confidence.

The teenager went in the office and came back out with Birdie, a burly guy with glasses. Birdie Farrell is pretty famous around town because he worked as a professional wrestler for awhile before opening Home Run Heaven. He was a "bad guy" wrestler, and when he was getting beaten up, the crowd would chant, "Bye Bye Birdie."

I never really liked Birdie, and I don't think he liked me either. One time me and a few other kids were in the store looking at cards, and Birdie accused me of shoplifting. I hadn't stolen anything, but he would watch me like a surveillance camera every time I came in. It seemed like Birdie took one too many head butts in his career, and it made him paranoid or something.

I tried to avoid the place if I could, but the nearest baseball-card store besides Birdie's was too far away to get to by bike.

Besides, Birdie would be able to authenticate the card for me. Somebody told me he used to have a T-206 Honus Wagner card framed on the wall of the store. When baseball-card prices were just starting to skyrocket and word got around how valuable the card was, Birdie took it down. I guess he sold it or swapped it or put it in a safe or something.

"What can I do for you, Stoshack?" Birdie said. I could tell from his voice and the look on his face that he really meant, "Why are you bothering me, Stoshack?"

I didn't say anything. I just opened my backpack

and carefully took out the Honus Wagner card. I placed it on the counter and watched Birdie's face.

His jaw dropped as soon as he saw it. His eyes opened wide, his eyebrows arching upward. I could see beads of sweat appear on his forehead.

"Where'd you get this?" he demanded.

"Found it."

"Found it where? Just lying on the street?"

"Sorta."

The teenager who had been snotty to me was now looking at me as if Elvis had walked into the store. He leaned over to get a good look at the card, but Birdie took out a magnifying glass and pushed the teenager's head away roughly.

Birdie peered at the card for nearly a minute. He carefully turned it over with a pair of tweezers and examined the other side. Finally, he lifted his eyes and met mine. He had regained his composure.

"I know what you're thinking, kid," he said to me. "You think you found a 1909 Honus Wagner T-206. Well, you've got an authentic Wagner here all right, but it's *Heinie* Wagner, not Honus Wagner. Heinie Wagner was another Pirate in the same card set. I hate to bust your bubble, but there are *thousands* of cards just like this one floating around."

My heart dropped like a bungee jumper.

"Are you sure?" I asked, almost pleading for him to say no.

"Positive," Birdie said. "Tell you what. You're a nice kid. I'll give you ten dollars for it."

I was crushed. I had already begun making plans for how I would spend the thousands of dollars I would get for the card. And then it turned out to be worth next to nothing.

I considered Birdie's offer. Maybe I should take the money, I thought. Ten bucks is ten bucks, and that would make twenty dollars I'd earned for the day. Not bad.

"So do we have a deal?" Birdie asked, sticking out his hand for me to shake. The snotty teenager watched silently.

I looked Birdie in the eye. He was sweating like crazy. I could see it right through his shirt. Why was he acting so nervous about a simple ten-dollar deal? I wondered.

Suddenly, I realized that Birdie was lying to me. Heinie Wagner wasn't on the Pittsburgh Pirates. He played for the Boston Red Sox. The guy on this card had "PITTSBURG" across his chest and the only Pirate of that era named Wagner was the great Honus Wagner.

"No," I finally said. "I think I'll see what another dealer has to say."

"Wait," Birdie said urgently. "I'll give you one hundred dollars."

"I thought you said the card was worth ten dollars."

"One thousand dollars," Birdie said desperately. "I'll give you one thousand dollars. Cash. Right here, right now. I've got the money in the back."

"Thanks for your honesty and your generous offer, Birdie," I said in my best sarcastic voice. "I'll just take one of these protective cardholders."

I flipped two quarters on the counter and carefully inserted the card between the two sheets of clear plastic. I slipped the card inside my wallet and put the wallet in my backpack. Birdie was watching me carefully, fuming. He doesn't like it when twelve-year-old kids make a chump out of him. But I didn't care. Having the card gave me the confidence to turn down Birdie's offer.

As I was leaving Home Run Heaven, the snotty teenager followed me out the door.

"Hey kid!" he yelled as I threw my leg over my bike. He came over to me and leaned close to my ear.

"Let me give you some advice," he said. "Word's gonna get around. Put the card in a safe place, and do it fast. That's the most valuable piece of cardboard in the world, and a lot of people would like to have it."

I didn't like the sound of that.

I FIGURED THAT BEFORE I DID ANYTHING ELSE WITH THE card, I'd better do some homework on Honus Wagner. I pedaled south down Third Street to the Ekstrom Library at the University of Louisville to see what I could dig up.

There weren't any books about Honus Wagner, but almost every baseball book mentioned him. I knew Wagner was a Hall of Famer, but I never knew how great he really was.

Just for starters, he was one of the best hitters in baseball history. He hit over .300 for seventeen straight years. He won the National League batting championship eight times, and four times in a row.

Despite his size, he could run like a scared rabbit. Wagner stole 722 bases over his career, and led the league in stolen bases five times. Ty Cobb stole more bases, but Wagner averaged more steals per time

27

reaching first than Cobb did, .213 to .207. Those are stats the average fan would miss.

He could field like an octopus. Shortstop is the toughest position to play, so managers usually put their best fielder there. Every baseball book said that Wagner was undisputably the greatest shortstop ever.

His hands were enormous, nearly as big as the gloves they used to wear in those days. Wagner would charge ground balls like a bull and scoop them up like a shovel. He grabbed handfuls of dirt along with the ball, so when the throw reached its target, the first baseman would be pelted by rocks and pebbles. It was like the tail of a comet.

They say his throws were always accurate from wherever he threw. He would pick up grounders down the leftfield line that got past the third baseman, and then throw the runner out at first with time to spare. One book said he threw out baserunners while lying on his back.

In 1908, Wagner totally dominated the National League. He won the batting title with a .354 average, when the entire league hit just .239. He also led in hits, doubles, triples, runs batted in, on-base average, total bases, slugging percentage, and stolen bases. Just about the only categories he didn't lead the league in were runs and home runs. He finished second in those.

Some season!

In fact, many baseball experts think Honus Wagner was the greatest all-around player in the history of the game.

Interestingly, almost every baseball book mentioned that Wagner was funny-looking. He was sort of ugly and awkward. He didn't look like a typical ballplayer.

He reminded me of *me* a little bit. I wondered if kids made fun of him when he was growing up. I wished I could meet him and ask him.

There was one last thing I wanted to look up—the value of the T-206 Honus Wagner baseball card.

The Louisville Library gets *The New York Times,* so I scanned the index for WAGNER, HONUS. There was nothing listed for 1995, 1994, 1993, or 1992, but in 1991 the paper ran one article that mentioned Honus Wagner. The index said it appeared in the March 23, 1991 edition. I went to the microfilm department and put in a request for that date.

A few minutes later the librarian gave me a reel of microfilm. I threaded it through the machine and advanced the film to March 23rd. I turned to the sports section of that day, and there it was . . .

DAN GUTMAN

Honus Wagner Baseball Card Goes to Gretzky

By RITA REIF

A multicolored baseball card depicting Honus Wagner, the great shortstop for the Pittsburg Pirates, was sold yesterday for $451,000 to Wayne Gretzky, the Los Angeles Kings hockey great, and Bruce McNall, the club's owner. The purchase, at Sotheby's in New York, represented the highest price paid at auction for sporting memorabilia, about four times the previous record, set in 1989 for another Honus Wagner card.

Issued by tobacco producers in 1909 and 1910, the Wagner cards are scarce because Wagner opposed smoking and objected to his name being linked to the cigarettes advertised on the backs of the cards. Only 40 cards depicting Wagner are known to exist; the one sold yesterday was described by Sotheby's as being in "mint condition."

A noise came out of my throat that must have sounded really weird, because everybody in the library turned to look at me.

Four hundred and fifty-one thousand dollars! I never would have *dreamed* the card was worth *that* much.

Alongside the short article there was a picture of the baseball card Wayne Gretzky had purchased. It was identical to the card in my backpack. I was sitting on almost a half a million dollars.

I'm not quite sure if I pedaled my bike home from the library or if it just floated on a cushion of air.

What could I do with a half a million dollars? Well, first I'd buy my mom a house in the nice part of town, and a car that didn't break down every few months. I would finally get a computer for my room, and some cool software. I could put some money away for college. My mom could quit her job, of course.

Without any money problems, Mom and Dad would probably fall back in love and we'd be a family again. We'd hire some servants to do the shopping and cooking and cleaning and all the other stuff Mom hates to do.

And after all that, I'd buy every baseball card that was ever printed.

As I pedaled home, I felt like the luckiest kid in the world. I also felt a funny feeling all over. It was the tingling sensation, but more than that. I felt a presence, a mysterious feeling that somebody was *with* me. I couldn't quite figure it out, but I would soon.

ONE LAST PEEK

7

I WAS DYING TO TELL MOM ABOUT THE CARD, BUT I WASN'T sure how to handle it. Mom's a bit of a goody-two-shoes about doing the right thing all the time. She might do something crazy like force me to give the card back to Miss Young. I almost busted a gut trying to hold back the news during dinner.

"Is something bothering you, Joe?" Mom asked as we scraped our plates off into the garbage.

"I'm just excited about my ballgame tomorrow, Mom," I lied.

"Who are you playing?"

"The Galante Giants."

"Those lunatics?"

"Yeah."

I did my homework and watched some TV after dinner before crawling into bed. Just before clicking off the light, I opened my backpack and took out the

32

Wagner card. I wanted to look at it one more time before I went to sleep.

The tingling sensation started as I held the card in my hand. It was a pleasant, buzzy feeling, like a cat purring in my ear.

My eyes felt droopy. I was thinking about Honus Wagner and what a great player he was. I was wondering if he was that good when he was a kid, and if the other kids made fun of him because he looked funny. I wished I could meet him.

That was the last thing I remembered before dropping off to sleep.

Sometime during the night there was a stirring in my room. I thought for a moment it was the house creaking, but the sound was loud enough to make me sit up in bed out of a deep sleep.

I jumped. Air escaped from my mouth in a startled gasp. I brought my hand to my mouth to cover it. My eyes were wide and they strained to adjust to the light from my night table.

There was a man in my room. He was sitting in the chair at my desk, calmly watching me. He didn't look like he was a thief robbing the house. He was wearing a baseball uniform.

"Who are you?" I asked, dumbfounded.

"Who are *you?*" he replied softly.

"Joe. Joe Stoshack. My friends call me Stosh."

"Then that's what I'll call you. Pleased to meet you, Stosh." He stood up and stuck out his right hand to shake. The hand was enormous, about the size of a canned ham. It enveloped mine completely, but gently.

I looked the guy over. He was a big man. Not tall, but solid. About 200 pounds. He must have been in his mid-thirties, sort of weird-looking, with big ears and a big nose. There were bags under his brown eyes, and a tinge of sadness in his face. He somehow reminded me of Abraham Lincoln.

As he sat back down in the chair, I could see his legs were bowed like mine, but even worse. His chest seemed to be as big as a barrel. There was plenty of room on it for the letters PITTSBURG. There was no H at the end.

"Honus . . . Wagner?" I whispered, rhyming "Honus" with "bonus."

"Honus," he said, rhyming it with "honest." "My friends call me Hans. It's from the German name Johannes."

"Am I dreaming?" I asked.

"I don't know," he said. "Maybe *I* am. Sure doesn't feel like a dream though, does it?"

"No. I just went to sleep, and when I woke up you were sitting here in my room."

"And I was at the ballpark shagging flies, and the next thing I knew I was here."

*   *   *

He was sort of weird-looking, with big ears and a big nose. There were bags under his brown eyes, and a tinge of sadness in his face.

Wait a minute! Shaking the sleep from my eyes, it occurred to me that this had to be some kind of trick. I'm no fool, and I know not to talk to strangers. I glanced around the room trying to locate my baseball bat. Maybe I could defend myself with it if I had to.

"Who *are* you, anyway?" I demanded.

"I already told you, Stosh," he replied gently. "Hans Wagner."

"If you're really Wagner, let's see you prove it," I said. "Show me some identification."

"Stosh, I don't carry my wallet in my uniform," the guy said calmly. "I have no way to prove to you who I am."

"Well, *I* do." I pulled my copy of *The Baseball Encyclopedia* out of the bookshelf and furiously flipped the pages until I reached the entry for Honus Wagner. "Okay *Honus,* or whatever your name is. What was your batting average in 1900?"

"That was my best year," he answered proudly. "I hit .381."

He was right.

"Yeah, well what's your birthday?" I asked.

"February 24th," he replied. "1874."

Anybody posing as Wagner would know that. I looked down the column for a more obscure statistic. "How many errors did you make in 1909?"

"That's easy," he said. "Forty-nine. But at least ten

of 'em should've been scored as hits, if you ask me. I couldn't have reached 'em with a butterfly net."

I still wasn't convinced the guy was Honus Wagner. "How many home runs did you hit in your career?" I asked.

He thought about that for a moment. "I can't answer that one, Stosh."

"If you're *really* Honus Wagner, why don't you know how many home runs you hit?"

"Well," he said, shaking his head. "I haven't *hit* 'em all yet. I hope I haven't anyway. I was countin' on playin' for a few more seasons before this old body is too beat up to hit homers."

"What *year* do you think this is?" I asked him.

"Why, it's 1909, of course," he responded. "What year do you think it is?"

I went over to my desk, picked up my calendar, and handed it to him.

"Jumpin' Jehoshaphat!" He was genuinely shocked. "Are you saying you traveled through time from 1909 to now?"

"I didn't say nothin', Stosh. But it sure looks like it."

"I thought time travel was just something on TV."

"TV?" he said, puzzled. "What's TV?"

"Never mind. Why are you here?" I asked.

"I don't know, Stosh. All I know is, somethin' very powerful brought me to you. You and me gotta figure

out what it is, and we gotta figure it out by tomorrow
'cause I got a big game on Saturday and I don't want
to miss it. I gotta get back to 1909."

This guy put on a good act, but I still wasn't *en-
tirely* convinced it was Honus Wagner. It was just too
weird to think that he traveled through time and
landed in my bedroom.

Suddenly, I remembered the card. Where was it?
Frantically, I pulled the blankets off my bed. It
wasn't there.

"Where is it?" I almost yelled at him.

"Where is *what?*" he replied gently.

I turned around and threw my pillow aside. The
card was right there, still in its plastic case.

Honus looked at the card, shook his head, and
chuckled as he watched me. "You okay, Stosh?"

"*I* know." I turned to him slowly and pointed my finger
at him. "You were trying to steal my card! That's what
happened. You dressed up as Honus Wagner, snuck into
my house, and tried to trick me into thinking I was having a dream! Who hired you, Birdie Farrell?"

"Hired me? Stosh, why would anybody steal a baseball card?"

The way he said that, it was obvious he honestly
didn't know the answer.

"This baseball card could solve a lot of my problems," I told him.

"Son, no piece of cardboard is gonna solve a man's problems, unless it's to keep a draft out of his window."

"What if I told you this card was worth a half a million dollars?"

"I'd say you're loony," Honus said. "They give those things away for free."

"Maybe in 1909 they did," I explained. "Today they're worth a fortune."

He laughed again, like I was putting him on.

"Do you have any idea how much they pay baseball players today?" I asked him.

"Oh, I don't know, Stosh. The cost of everything is always going up. $20,000? $30,000 maybe?"

"The average major league salary is a *million* dollars a year. If you were playing today, you'd get *six* million. Maybe more."

"Now I'm *sure* you're loony. Son, when I broke into the majors, I was paid two hundred fifty dollars a month. And that was *good* money! Heck, a mug o' root beer only cost a few pennies. Last season I held out until old man Dreyfuss coughed up $10,000. With that, I'm satisfied. Ten grand is as much money as *any* man should be paid to throw and hit a ball."

I sat back down on my bed. This guy actually *was* Honus Wagner, I realized.

I always had a special feeling about baseball cards, and now I understood what that feeling was. A baseball card, for me, could be like a time machine. With a 1909 Honus Wagner card in my hand, I *wished* I could meet Honus, and he traveled through time to fulfill my wish.

Cool!

If a baseball card could be a time machine, the possibilities were unlimited. I could get a Ty Cobb baseball card and bring back The Georgia Peach. Or Jackie Robinson. Or "Shoeless" Joe Jackson.

Why, I could bring Babe Ruth to my bedroom to talk about his glory years with the Yankees! I could bring The Sultan of Swat to school for show and tell! I'd just need his baseball card.

Honus interrupted my reverie. "You play ball, Stosh?"

"Yeah, but I'm no good," I admitted. I told him how kids made fun of the way I look and how it throws me off when I'm trying to hit or field.

"They used to give it to me bad," Honus said, putting his hands on his bowed legs. "Kids used to say that I was the only person in the world who could tie his shoelaces without bending down. They used to say that if I ever straightened my legs out, I'd be seven feet tall. That sort of thing. One guy said you could roll a barrel through my legs. But let me tell you something." He leaned closer to me. "They could never roll a *baseball* through my legs."

"What did you do when kids said that kind of stuff?"

"Simple. I'd hit a single. Then I'd steal second. Then I'd steal third. Then I'd steal home. Then they'd shut up."

"That's easy for you," I said sadly, "You're Honus Wagner."

Honus leaned over to me again. He was almost whispering. "Y'know, Stosh, you remind me a little of *me* as a boy. You even look like me. You've got the tools to be a good player. You just have to convince yourself."

"Sure . . ."

The old pep talk. I'd heard it a million times. I was sick of it. Some people are just born athletes, I had convinced myself, and others are born to do something else. I was born to do something else.

"Stosh, do you want to know the one secret to bein' a great ballplayer?"

"Don't tell me, let me guess," I said. "Keep your eye on the ball?"

"Nah, any monkey can do that," Honus said. "The secret to bein' a great ballplayer—" He looked around the room as if he didn't want anyone else to hear, "is to trick yourself into thinkin' you already are one."

"Huh?"

"It's the same with anything, Stosh. The secret to bein' a great barber is to trick yourself into thinkin' you already are one. The secret to bein' a great salesman is to trick yourself into thinkin' you already are one. And once you think you are one, you *become* one. See what I mean?"

I couldn't say that I did. But who was I to tell the great Honus Wagner he wasn't making any sense?

Honus went on, spinning old baseball stories late into the night. I felt myself getting drowsy, but fought it off the best I could. If this is only a dream, I thought to myself, I don't want to miss a minute of it.

Eventually my eyelids became too heavy, and I fell into a deep sleep. I hadn't even thought to ask him for his autograph.

DAYDREAMING

WHEN I WOKE UP IN THE MORNING, HONUS WAS GONE. "IT must have just been a dream," I thought to myself.

But if it was a dream, it was the most vivid dream I ever had. *The Baseball Encylopedia* was on the floor next to my bed. It was open to the page with Honus Wagner on it.

I stuck the Wagner card in my backpack and got ready for school. I wasn't about to let the card out of my sight for a second.

It was impossible to concentrate at school. I couldn't get Honus or the card out of my head. Should I sell it? Keep it? Give it back to Miss Young? Did I really have the power to bring people through time with baseball cards, or didn't I? I didn't know.

I was daydreaming about all this stuff during math class when I suddenly heard Mrs. Kelly call my name.

"Mr. Stoshack, can you tell us the answer?"

"Uh . . ." I guessed. "Four?"

The class roared with laughter.

"Joe, the question was, 'What is one-tenth of two thousand?' I'm going to assume that you knew the answer but your mind was elsewhere, okay?"

"Thanks, Mrs. Kelly." She was a pretty-all-right lady for a teacher.

"Good, Joe. Now let's try and focus on what we're doing."

But I couldn't. I don't think I learned much at school that day.

"Nobatternobatternobatternobatternobatternobatter . . ."

The Galante Giants are a strange bunch. The team is sponsored by the Galante Funeral Home. The black uniforms don't bother anybody, but they make a big show out of carrying their bats to their games in a fake coffin. People decided the Giants were *really* weird when they started bringing a tombstone to their games and putting the name of the opposing team on it.

The Giants are also really good players. With most teams, every time there's a fly ball to the outfield, three or four guys run out there, bonk heads, and the ball drops right between them. The Giants are careful to call "I got it." They know their signals. They always throw to the right base. They never forget how many outs there are.

They had us 7-4 going into the sixth inning. Our first two guys struck out and the game looked hopeless. But their pitcher walked a couple of guys, and Billy Shields cracked a double down the rightfield line to score both of them. That made it 7-6. Billy was on second base. A single would tie it up.

Johnny Conlon was due up, but he had a dentist appointment and his mom took him home at the end of the fifth inning. Coach looked up and down the bench for a pinch hitter. I hadn't been in the game yet, and every kid is supposed to play at least one inning.

I slunk down into my seat. I had fanned to end the last game, and I didn't want to make a habit of it.

"Stoshack," Coach yelled, "Grab a bat."

Shoot!

Somebody groaned when Coach called my name, and I couldn't say I blamed him. Everybody knew I couldn't hit. Putting me up there in this situation was like throwing the game away.

I decided I wasn't going to swing no matter what. If you don't swing, you can't miss. Maybe he'll walk me, I figured. He's walked two guys already this inning. Somebody else can make the last out.

The Giant's pitcher looked in for the sign, nodded, and threw. It was right down the middle of the plate, nice and easy.

"Steeeerikkkke one!" yelled the ump.

Maybe he's on to me, I thought. He knows I'm not swinging, so he's going to throw it right over. I swung my bat menacingly and put a determined look on my face. Gotta pretend I'm gonna take a rip at this one.

Once again the pitcher got the sign and threw a marshmallow right down Broadway.

"Steeeerikkkke two!" yelled the ump.

Two strikes. I stepped out of the batter's box. He definitely knows I'm taking all the way. He's gonna lay it right over the plate again. That'll be strike three and the end of the game.

That's it, I said to myself. I'm swinging.

I thought about what Honus had told me. The way to be a great player is to pretend you already *are* one. I closed my eyes and tried to imagine I had hit a home run in my last at-bat, and I was the league's Most Valuable Player. Nobody could throw a pitch by me.

I got back in the box and gave the pitcher my meanest glare.

"Drive me in, Stosh!" Billy hollered from second as he stretched his lead.

"Tie it up, Joe!" somebody yelled from our bench.

"Stoshack, we're gonna *bury* you!" one of their guys screamed.

"We're gonna *murder* you!"

I let all the air out of my lungs to get relaxed. My

bat was nearly straight up and down. I held it firmly, but not so tight that I wouldn't be able to turn my wrists. My weight was on my back leg.

The pitcher looked in for the sign, but I knew what he was going to throw. A cream puff right down the middle. That's exactly what I saw—a big, fat, juicy, slow ball, just right for whacking over a wall.

"Hey!" somebody yelled as I pulled the trigger, "Noodle nose!"

I brought my arms around, swiveling my hips, shifting my weight forward, and whipping the bat head across the plate. Bat and ball met, with the bat kissing the ball an inch below its equator. The ball soared almost straight up in the air.

"Run, Stosh!"

I took off for first. Billy, running on anything, dashed for third. It looked like it would be a fair ball, and it looked like it would never come down.

The Giant's catcher ripped his mask off his face and tossed it aside. He took two steps forward into fair territory and planted his feet. The ball reached it's highest point and started coming down. I reached first and turned around to watch. Billy was steaming around third and charging home. If the catcher makes the play the game is over. If he can't hold on to the ball, Billy scores and we tie the game.

Plop.

The ball settled in the catcher's glove. Three outs.

Game over. We lose. At least I didn't whiff, I thought, as I trudged back to the bench.

"Woulda been a home run," the catcher said as I passed him, "if we were playing in an elevator shaft."

The team got in a line, shook hands with the Giants, and everybody scattered to go home. I packed up my duffel bag with my bat, glove, and a bunch of balls. I was about to leave when I heard somebody call to me.

"You're overstriding," a man's voice said. "That's why you got under the ball."

I turned around. It was Honus, sitting on the steps in street clothes, with a dog on each side of him and a bag behind him.

"It *wasn't* a dream!" I shouted, giving him a big hug. "You're really here!"

"Or if it was a dream, we must both still be dreamin'."

I was so happy to see him. I was bursting with questions. "When did you leave last night? Where did you go? Where did you sleep?"

"Whoa! Slow down, Stosh. I guess I was borin' you with my stories, 'cause you fell asleep right in the middle of one of 'em. So I climbed out your window. I walked the streets a bit and I slept right here."

"You slept in the field?"

"Stosh, I slept in plenty of fields in my time."

I turned around. It was Honus.

"Where'd you get those clothes? You look pretty good!"

"Thanks. Somebody was throwin' 'em away and I grabbed 'em just before the garbage man came down the street. Thought I'd look pretty strange walkin' around in my uniform."

"You must be starved, Honus. When's the last time you ate?"

"In 1909," he laughed. "I could use a bite."

There was a little luncheonette around the corner, and the dogs followed us there. I got a sandwich to go and a Pepsi to wash it down. He devoured the sandwich in about ten seconds as we walked by a vacant lot.

"Hey Stosh, wanna play some ball?"

"With you?!"

"Well, Ty Cobb ain't here, is he? Grab your glove."

I handed him my bat, and he looked at it strangely. "Ain't they got wood no more?" he asked.

"Yeah, but in Little League we use aluminum."

"Can't stop progress, I guess."

I ran out to the middle of the lot and Honus slapped a grounder at me. I scooped it up and fired it back to him. He smothered the ball in his huge hands. He slapped the next grounder a little to my left so I had to reach for it, and then another to my right so I had to backhand it. Each time I handled the ball cleanly.

He hit about a dozen grounders my way, and then a bunch of high pops. I nabbed nearly all of them, and when I didn't he'd shout, "Get down on the ball!" or "Charge it!"

"Not bad, Stosh," Honus shouted when he saw I was out of breath. "Now let me see you hit the ball."

I grabbed the bat and drew a strike zone on the cement wall with a rock.

"You can pitch?" I hollered as he paced off sixty feet.

"Heck, I twirl a few games when the regular pitchers are worn out. I don't have much of a curve, but I throw *hard*. They say if I ever hit a batter they should send for an undertaker, because it'll be too late for an ambulance."

Honus went into his windup and whipped the ball over. I could barely see it.

"Whoa! I'm only twelve, y'know!"

"Sorry!" He slowed it down a little on the next one, but all I hit was air. "Don't twist your body all up! Keep your feet planted!"

He threw another one and I fouled it off to the right.

"You're jerkin' your swing, Stosh! Smooth it out!"

After thirty swings or so, I was hitting the ball pretty good, and Honus was shouting, "Good!" "Better!" and, "Now you're hittin' like you mean it!"

We flopped down in the grass by a fence. Honus pulled up a big piece of grass and chewed on it. I did the same.

"Y'know, you ain't half bad, Stosh," he said. "You got a nice stroke. Who taught you to play, your dad?"

"Nah. I don't see my dad very much."

I told Honus about my parents splitting up, and how they used to argue about money all the time.

"At least you got two parents," Honus said. "My ma died when I was young. There were nine of us—five boys and four girls. There was no money to fight over. We were poor as dirt. By the time I was your age I was workin' in the coal mines along with my dad."

"They let kids work in coal mines?"

"*Let* 'em?!" he laughed. "*Made* 'em! During the winter we hardly saw daylight. We'd go in the mines before sunrise and didn't come out until night. There were rats all over the place, and they could sense when a cave-in was coming. When they ran for their lives, we ran for ours too."

"I bet it didn't pay a lot."

"Seventy cents a ton. It wasn't much, but it made me strong up here." He pounded his chest with his hand.

"So if you worked in the mines all the time, how did you become a ballplayer?"

"In the summer we brought our gloves with us, and at lunchtime we'd play a game. My brothers poked fun at me because I was clumsy. But I got better and grew bigger, and soon I was as good as any of 'em."

"Did any of your brothers make it to the majors?"

"Well Butts did for a year. But then he banged up his knee, and he was finished."

"Your brother's name is *Butts*?!"

"His real name's Albert, but everybody calls him Butts. It was Butts who got me into professional baseball. He was with Steubenville in 1895, and he told his manager that my *other* brother, Will, was a pretty good ballplayer. Will wasn't interested in playing ball professionally, but I was. Anything to get out of the mines. So when they offered Will a tryout, I hopped a freight train to Steubenville and took his place."

"They didn't know the difference?"

"Nah. Me and my brothers used to switch places all the time. We all pretty much look alike. Anyway, the manager didn't want to sign me, but Butts said he'd quit the team if I wasn't on it. So I joined the Steubenville team. I even signed the contract with Will's name. We played against teams like the Kalamazoo Kazoos. I hit about .400, stole a few bases, and played every position on the field."

"How did you get from Steubenville to the Pittsburgh Pirates?"

"Word got around about me, I guess. One day a bunch of us were chuckin' lumps of coal at an empty hopper across the Monongahela River. We spotted a guy watchin' us. We thought he was a cop, so we ran like the dickens. Turned out he was Ed Barrow, a scout."

"He signed you?"

"Not right away. I played cute, pretendin' I wasn't interested. Finally, Barrow says to me, 'Isn't there somethin' I can do for you? Isn't there somethin' you'd like to have?' I told him I'd like to have a bag of bananas. So he ran out, bought a bag of bananas, and gave it to me. How could I refuse him? I signed for thirty-five dollars a month and a bag of bananas. Next thing I knew I was in the big leagues playing for the Louisville Colonels.

"You played right here in Louisville?"

"For three years. They sold me to Pittsburgh in 1900, and I've been there ever since."

"What's it like playing in the big leagues, Honus?"

"Like bein' on the highest mountain, Stosh. It's all I ever dreamed of. I'd rather be shortstop for the Pittsburgh Pirates than President of the United States."

"That's my dream, too," I confided. "To play in the big leagues. Even if it was just for one at-bat. I just want to know what it feels like.

"You got the tools, Stosh."

"Do you have a dream *now,* Honus? Is there anything you want that you don't have?"

"To win the World Series," he said right away. "I played in the first one, in 1903. We won three of the first four games. But then our pitchin' gave out, and I couldn't hit a beach ball. Made six errors. Boston whupped us."

◄STEUBENVILLE BASE BALL CLUB►

❖ Inter State League ❖

Season of 1895.   Geo. L. Moreland, Manager

Sec. 1—This is to certify that I...William J. H. Wagner...

have agreed to play in the Steubenville Base Ball Club during the season of 1895
$35.00 (Thirty Five) per month payable on the first and fifteenth of each month or as soon
as possible.

Sec. 2—In signing to play for Steubenville team I agree to abide by all the Rules and Regulations.

Sec. 3—I also agree that should my services not be agreeable to the said club the Management
reserves the right to release me.

Sec. 4—I agree to pay for my own uniform and shoes, the cost of the same to be taken out of my
first Pay.

Sec. 5—I agree to report on the date notified by the Manager in good condition so as to play ball.

Sec. 6—The Manager of the Steubenville team to pay all my expenses while away from home.

Sec. 7—I also agree to always keep myself in good condition and should I fail to abide by all
rules, all agreements between myself and said Steubenville Club shall be declared void.

Received Feb. 10   Signed...William Wagner
1895.   Wittness...Patrick Flanahity
Geo. L. Moreland,
    Manager.   I played under the name
                        of William Wagner this year.
                                        J.H.W.

*My brother Will was a pretty good ballplayer. Will wasn't interested
in playing professionally, but I was. So when they gave Will a tryout,
I hopped a freight train to Steubenville and showed up in his place.*

His face suddenly looked serious.

"Y'know Stosh," he said, "as much as I enjoy your company, I can't stay here forever. We ain't figured out how to get me back. And I've got a game to play tomorrow."

"Well, I used the baseball card to bring you here," I said, "I should be able to send you back the same way."

"I was thinkin' about that Stosh. Can you go through time yourself, or just bring people back from the past?"

"I don't know," I admitted. "I'm still kinda new at this. Why?"

"Oh, I just had this crazy idea that I'd like to show you *my* time, if you could find a way to get there— and if you wanted to visit, of course."

"Me, go back to 1909?" I marvelled. "That would be cool! Let's try it."

"When?" he asked.

"Tonight, at my house. My mom will be asleep by ten o'clock."

"Ten it is." Honus stuck out his big hand and I shook it.

"Hey, what are you going to do until ten, Honus?" I asked.

"I don't know," he replied, "Go see a movie show or something."

"Do you have any money?"

He fished a few dimes out of his pocket and showed them to me.

"You can't buy a pack of *gum* with that, Honus!" I stuffed some bills in his hand, and he thanked me. Before he walked away I pulled my notebook out of my backpack and handed it to him with a pen.

"How much do you charge for autographs?" I asked.

"Charge?" said Honus, wrinkling his nose. "I figure kids should charge *us* 'cause they're nice enough to come watch us play."

He took the pen and wrote, "To my friend Stosh, Here's hoping both our dreams come true." And then he signed it . . .

Yours Sincerely

Honus Wagner

Honus turned to walk away again, but I called out to him.

"Hey Honus, is it true that once you hit a ball that went under the pitcher's arm and then it sailed over the centerfield fence for a home run?"

"You like that story?"

"Yeah."

"Then it's true. But that's nothin'. I was playin' in

Steubenville and this mutt would hang around the ballpark. I felt sorry for him, so I'd play fetch with him from time to time. One game I'm at short and a grounder trickled through my legs. The batter was roundin' first and headin' for second, when the mutt runs across the field. He snatched up the ball in his mouth and ran over to me. So I picked him up and tagged the runner with the dog. Ump called him out, too. How about that!"

"You made that up!"

"Did I ever lie to you?" he said with a twinkle in his eye. "There was this other time," he continued. "A guy hit a grounder right at me. But just as the ball was about to reach my glove, a rabbit ran across my path."

"What did you do?" I asked.

"Well, in the confusion, I picked up the rabbit and threw it to first."

"What happened?" I asked, incredulously.

"The ump called the runner out," Honus replied, pausing. "I got him by a hare."

With that, Honus slapped his knee and laughed uproariously.

"I'll see you at ten, Stosh," he said as he walked away.

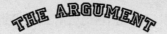

9

THE FIRST THING I DID WHEN I GOT HOME WAS TO OPEN my *Baseball Encyclopedia* and turn to "Wagner." I slid my finger up from "Honus" to "Heinie" to "Hal," and there it was . . .

Year	Team	Games	BA	SA	AB	H	2B	3B	HR	HR%	R	RBI	BB	SO	SB	Pinch Hit AB	Pinch Hit H	PO	A	E	DP	TC/G FA	G by Pos

Butts Wagner

WAGNER, ALBERT
  Brother of Honus Wagner
  B. Sept. 17, 1869, Mansfield, Pa D. Nov. 26, 1928, Pittsburg, Pa.
  BR TR 5'10", 170 lbs.

Year	Team	Games	BA	SA	AB	H	2B	3B	HR	HR%	R	RBI	BB	SO	SB	Pinch Hit AB	Pinch Hit H	PO	A	E	DP	TC/G	FA	G by Pos
1898	2 teams	WAS N (63G-.224)			BKN N (11G-.237)																			
•	total	74	.226	.307	261	59	12	3	1	0.4	22	34	16	4	1	0	97	126	46	9	3.6	.829		3B-50, OF-10, SS-8, 2B-5

I was reviewing the short career of Butts Wagner when Mom called me downstairs for dinner. I told her about the game, and then she dropped a bombshell.

"A Mr. Farrell called today, honey," she said. "From some baseball-card store. He says he wants to talk with you. What's going on?"

Uh-oh. Birdie Farrell. He wants the Honus Wagner card really badly. I could have simply lied and told Mom I didn't know what she was talking about. But in my experience, lies tend to catch up to you at some point. I decided to tell her the truth about the card.

"Something happened, Mom," I said awkwardly. She looked at me with concern as I pulled the Honus Wagner card out of my backpack. I told her how I found the card while cleaning out Miss Young's attic, how I authenticated it, and how I figured out how much it was worth. I didn't tell her about actually *meeting* Honus Wagner.

When I was finished, she let out a long whistle. "A half a million dollars?" she said, sitting down with a thud, "Are you sure?"

"I'm positive," I replied. "Mom, we're rich! We can get a new car! We can get out of this dump! I can go to college someday!"

Mom didn't look like one of those lottery winners they show on TV. She had a worried expression on her face, as if I had busted a neighbor's window or something. She sat there for a long time thinking before rendering her verdict.

"You have to give the card back to Miss Young,

Joe," she said seriously. "It's not yours to keep. And this house is not a dump."

"Are you crazy?!" I couldn't help but shout. "Mom, this is the solution to all our problems! And you want me to give it back? Miss Young doesn't even know I *have* the card! She doesn't even know it's *missing!* She probably didn't even know she ever had it in the first place!"

"Joe, it's the right thing to do, and you know it."

How stupid I was to tell her I found the card in Miss Young's attic! I should have told her I found it in the street or something.

I ran upstairs to my room and slammed the door behind me.

Dad came over later that night. He and Mom had some paperwork they had to go over. Usually when Dad comes over we spend some time together, but I was mad and didn't want to come out of my room.

I heard Dad ask Mom why I was upstairs. I couldn't make out Mom's response, but she must have told him about the baseball card.

Silently, I opened my bedroom door and crept to the edge of the stairs.

"It's wrong, Bill," Mom said. "It's as simple as that."

"Lots of things are wrong, Terry," Dad said. "Usually it's wrong and *we're* the losers. This time we can come out the winners."

"We?" Mom asked. "What do *you* have to do with this?"

"I gave him my baseball card collection, remember?" Dad said. "*I'm* the one who got him interested in collecting cards. I told him years ago that Wagner's card was the rarest one of all. If it weren't for me he would have thrown the card in the trash with the old lady's other junk."

Mom and Dad were getting steamed, just like they used to before Dad moved out.

"Look, Terry." Dad was going into his comforting mode. "Let's think this through together. The old lady will never know about the card. She told Joe to throw all the stuff out, didn't she? She's lived a full life. What's she going to do with all that money now? She has no relatives to give it to. The government is going to get the money when she dies. It's just common sense that we should sell the card. You've gotta admit you could do a few nice things with a half a million bucks."

I waited anxiously to hear Mom's response. She took a long time, as if she was carefully searching for the words she wanted.

"If we kept that card," she said softly, "we'd feel bad about it for the rest of our lives."

"If we give it back we'll feel bad about it for the rest of our lives!" Dad shouted.

*   *   *

I couldn't take it anymore. I stormed down the stairs and shouted at the two of them.

"It's *my* card. *I* found it. Doesn't anybody care what *I* want to do with it?"

They stared at me.

"Hey, Joey," Dad said, embarrassed. "What are you doing out of bed?"

"Joseph." Mom always called me Joseph when she was about to say something she knew I didn't want to hear. "When you're a grown-up, you can make important decisions yourself. But for now, we do that for you. And I've decided that card belongs to Miss Young."

Dad turned away disgustedly. I stormed back upstairs, shouting, "That's not fair!" before slamming the door.

"I just won't give it to her," I thought, "I'm gonna put the card somewhere Mom'll *never* find it."

I took the card out of my knapsack. Then I turned off the light and waited.

At ten o'clock, right on schedule, there was a tap on my window. Honus climbed in the room.

"Ready for a little time travelin' tonight, partner?" he asked.

"You bet, Hans!"

As he took off his street clothes and pulled on his

uniform, Honus noticed my baseball card collection next to my bed. He picked it up and flipped the plastic pages.

"All these cards worth a half a million bucks?" he asked.

"No, only yours," I explained. "When you said you didn't want your name and face to be associated with a tobacco product, it drove up the price of the cards they'd already printed."

"Everybody chewed or smoked in my day," Honus said as he turned a page.

"I read somewhere that you didn't object to smoking. You were just mad because they didn't pay you to use your picture."

"That's bull," he said sharply. "It's a disgustin' habit, settin' fire to leaves and suckin' 'em down your throat. Didn't want to be responsible for kids doin' that. Besides, a kid shouldn't have to buy somethin' to get a picture of me. Should be free."

"Smoking causes all kinds of diseases, you know," I informed him.

"Didn't take no genius to figure that out, I hope."

Honus stopped at one page and peered closely at a card. "So they finally let colored boys into the game, eh?"

"In 1947. A guy named Jackie Robinson was the first. They're called 'African-Americans' now." I felt proud that I could tell him something he didn't know.

"African-Americans, huh? You know who was the greatest shortstop I ever saw?" Honus asked. "A guy named John Henry Lloyd."

"Never heard of him."

"He played in the Negro Leagues. They used to call him The Black Wagner. But I'll tell you, I would have considered it an honor to be called The White Lloyd. That guy could suck grounders up like a magnet. It's a crime the way they don't let those boys play with us. The smartest pitcher I saw was another colored fella, a guy named Rube Foster."

"He made it to Cooperstown eventually," I told Honus.

"Cooperstown?" Honus asked innocently. "What league is that in?"

"Never mind."

"This Barry Bonds," he said, pointing to a card. "Is he any good?"

"One of the best. Makes over five million a year."

"Didn't ask how much he makes. Asked if he was any good."

"Sure. He hit .311 in 1992. For your Pirates, in fact."

".311?" Wagner snorted. "For *my* Pirates, he'd be a benchwarmer."

"It's a different game now, Hans. They play indoors, on artificial turf. They use the DH."

"DH?"

"Designated hitter," I explained. "It's a player who hits in the pitcher's place but doesn't play the field. They only have them in the American League."

"That ain't baseball," Honus grumbled. "In baseball, a man hits, fields, runs, and throws. If he can't do those four things, he should get himself a desk job."

It was time to get down to business. I grabbed my backpack and lay down on my bed with the card in my hand, closing my eyes.

"Think of 1909," Honus said as he leaned over me, " 'cause that's where I gotta be by three o'clock tomorrow afternoon. Feel anything happening, Stosh?"

"Yeah," I replied sleepily. "Powerful tingles. Hey Honus, do you think this was all a dream?"

"I don't know," Honus said, "But if I miss the game, it'll be a nightmare."

My body felt weary. I still couldn't get my mom's words out of my mind. *When you're a grown-up, you can make important decisions yourself.* I wished I was a grown-up.

"Hey Honus?" I asked as my eyelids fell like the huge curtains in a theater.

"Yeah, Stosh?"

"In 1909, is everything in black and white?"

"Of course not, Stosh," Honus laughed.

"Well, I've seen pictures of those times and everything looks black and white."

"The past is in color, Stosh! Beautiful color. You should see it."

I wish I could, I thought. *I wish I could.*

10

DAYLIGHT STREAMING IN THE WINDOW SNUCK THROUGH MY eyelids and awakened me. It must have just been another dream, I thought, and now it's over.

I lay there with my eyes closed thinking about how wonderful it had been. I tried to recall everything Honus had said, because I usually forget my dreams as soon as I wake up in the morning. My body felt different, somehow.

I figured I'd better get up. I rolled over on my side to check the clock on my night table. One o'clock! Mom never lets me sleep so late, even on Saturday. My mind scrambled to figure out what was going on.

Wait a minute! The clock had *hands*. I have a *digital* clock. I bolted from the bed and looked around the room.

It wasn't my room!

There was flowery wallpaper on the walls and a

landscape painting in a fancy frame. It wasn't a kid's room. The room was filled with antiques. All the furniture was made of wood. There were two beds. The other one looked like it had been slept in, too. My sneakers, clothes, and backpack were on the floor. I must have taken them off during the night.

I opened the night table drawer. Inside was a Bible and some sheets of blank stationery. "Pontchartrain Hotel, Detroit, Michigan," it said at the top.

There was noise outside the window, so I got up to have a look. A bunch of antique cars were on the street, sputtering, backfiring, and honking their horns.

Across the street was a ballpark. There was a large sign on the front of it—BENNETT PARK. Never heard of it. People were streaming toward the ballpark. They were all wearing hats. The ladies wore enormous ones with flowers on them. It was really weird.

A door opened behind me. I turned around and Honus clomped into the room in his Pirate uniform, spikes and all. He was carrying a shaving brush and a towel. He didn't seem nearly as big as he did before.

Honus looked startled when he saw me. "Stosh?" he asked, as if he wasn't sure it was me.

"I guess I *can* travel through time, huh?" I said.

The voice coming out of my mouth didn't sound like me. It was lower. I noticed that Honus was looking me over carefully, up and down.

A bunch of antique cars were on the street . . . honking their horns. Across the street was a ballpark.

"Why are you staring at me like that, Honus?"

"Take a look in the mirror, Stosh."

There was a full-length mirror on the door. I walked over to it and was rocked back on my heels when I saw the image. The person in the mirror wasn't a twelve-year-old boy. It was a *man*. A man who was a bit under six feet tall, with large ears and bowed legs. The face looked pretty much like mine, but the body was that of a grown-up.

I was hairy in places where my skin used to be smooth. My breath tasted bad in my mouth. I smelled.

Suddenly I realized what had happened—I went to sleep with the baseball card wishing I could be a grown-up . . . and then I *became* one!

My face felt itchy. I touched it with my hand. I needed a shave. The floor looked farther away than usual, the ceiling closer.

I moved my arms and legs to prove to myself that the image in the mirror was really me and not some guy standing behind a sheet of glass.

Honus came over and stood behind me. We looked like we could be twin brothers.

"Kids sure grow up fast these days, huh Stosh? Y'know, you look like a real ballplayer now."

I made a muscle with my arm and tensed it. The bicep jumped up, like it does on those guys in the bodybuilding magazines. I started doing poses in the mirror.

"We'd better get movin' Stosh. I'll be late for batting practice."

"What year is this?"

Honus went over to the bureau, picked up a small calendar, and handed it to me. The front sheet had the word "October" at the top in large letters. Underneath, in smaller numbers, it said "1909."

"So it worked!" I said, marvelling at my new power. "Honus, where are we?"

"Detroit," he said with a laugh. He tossed me some of his clothes. "Put these on. Your stuff don't fit no more. Put on this jacket, too. It's a cold day."

I put on the clothes, and was careful to put the card back in my backpack.

"Where are we going, Honus?"

"To the game, of course," he replied.

"Why'd you put on your uniform in the hotel?" I asked as I grabbed my backpack and followed Honus down several flights of stairs. "Why not dress in the locker room?"

"No hot water. Besides, the kranks like to see us on their way to the game. Gets 'em riled up, you know?"

"Kranks?" I asked.

"Fanatics," Honus said as he pushed open the door facing the street. "Fans. Don't let the Tiger kranks bother you."

"*Detroit* Tiger kranks?"

"Yup. They're harmless."

"But Detroit's not in the National League," I said, confused. "The Pirates don't play the Tigers."

"In the World Series we do."

"This is the World *Series*?!" I said, stopping in the middle of the sidewalk.

"Told you I had a big game today." Honus threw an arm around my shoulder and hustled me past the cars whizzing down Trumbull Avenue toward the ballpark.

I was glad Honus told me to put on a jacket, because it was raw and windy outside. Terrible baseball weather.

But in front of Bennett Park it was like a county fair. The smell of roasted peanuts hung in the air. Red, white, and blue bunting hung around the ballpark. Band music blared in the distance. Cars coughed and trolleys clanked down the street. Newsboys hawked papers for a penny.

There was a sign on the front gate—BOTTLE THROWING WILL NOT BE TOLERATED!

"Hey Honus, good luck today!" somebody shouted as we walked past the ticket window. A hand-lettered sign over the booth indicated that box seats were selling for $1.25 and bleacher seats 75¢.

"Cobb's gonna run all over you, Dutchman!" a guy hooted at Honus.

"Mr. Wagner," asked a lady with a small boy. "Can you sign this for my son?" Honus stopped and took the lady's fountain pen. I noticed the boy was wearing a badge that read, "YOU MIGHT TY COBB, BUT YOU CAN'T TIE WAGNER." Honus used her son's head as a table to sign the lady's scorecard . . .

Honus Wagner

"Are you a ballplayer, too?" she asked, holding the pen out for me.

"No, I'm—"

"He's my brother," Honus said, throwing me a wink.

"Butts!" yelled a guy waiting in line. "Butts Wagner!"

"Hey Butts, how ya' doin'?"

"Haven't seen you in years, Butts! How's the knee?"

People gathered around us, clapping me on the back. Honus laughed as I greeted everyone as his brother and told them my knee was much better. The lady was still holding the scorecard and pen out for me, so I took them and wrote . . .

Best wishes!
Albert "Butts" Wagner

Honus whistled to get the attention of a guard, and whispered something in his ear. The guard handed him something and escorted us past the gate. Hans led me to a quiet tunnel under the ballpark.

"I've got a ducat for you, Stosh," Honus said, handing me a ticket. "Enjoy the game."

"Good luck, Honus."

"Thanks. Stosh, I got an idea this morning. I want you to watch me when I come off the field after each inning. If I look toward you and do this"— he patted his right shoulder with his left hand "—then you come down and meet me here right away. Got that?"

I patted my right shoulder with my left hand to make sure I had the sign.

"Okay, but why?" I was bewildered.

"It's a surprise," Honus said. "Oh, one more thing. Here's two bits. Get yourself some frankfurters or something. You'll get hungry." He flipped me a quarter.

"I'll pay you back," I promised.

"Forget it," he replied. "You fed me, now I'll feed you."

"Honus, this is a dream come true for me."

"Not yet it ain't."

With that, he hurried through a door marked VISI-TOR'S ENTRANCE.

11

THE SEAT WAS A GOOD ONE, RIGHT NEAR FIRST BASE AND A couple of rows off the field. It was made of wood. The floor was made of wood, too. Come to think of it, I noticed, *everything* was made of wood.

I scoped out the place. Bennett Park was much smaller than the ballparks I'd visited. The outfield fence was plastered with billboards—LA AZORA: THE CIGAR OF CIGARS. 50 TO EVERY PLAYER SCORING A HOME RUN. Everything from soda pop to clothing to dandruff treatments were being advertised.

People were hanging all over the fence, and there were seats in *front* of the fence. The only thing keeping fans away from the playing field was a rope. There was no warning track. I wondered how they handled home runs. Did outfielders just chase deep fly balls into the crowd?

Or maybe there were *no* deep fly balls. This was, I

realized, still the "dead ball era." Baseballs didn't travel very far. I remembered from reading baseball history books that in 1911 a livelier ball with a cork center was introduced.

The place was jammed with fans, and it seemed like all of them were waving a pennant, tooting a horn, or ringing a bell. Some people brought pots and pans to the ballpark, and they were banging on them with big spoons. People were even sitting on rickety bleachers set up on the rooftops of houses across the street from the ballpark.

It was cloudy and cold enough that the umpire was wearing an overcoat. I didn't mind the weather. I was getting to see the 1909 World Series!

There were no dugouts. Some of the players sat on a long bench, while the rest were warming up, snapping baseballs back and forth smartly. Their gloves were hardly any bigger than their hands, I noticed.

After a few minutes I saw Honus on the Pittsburgh bench. A photographer led him over to one of the Tigers and began shooting pictures of the two men as they compared their batting grips.

The seats next to me weren't filled yet, so I turned around and asked the two women in the row behind me, "Excuse me, is that Ty Cobb?"

"You must be from out of town, mister," one of them said. "Of *course* it's the great Cobb!"

A photographer led Honus over to one of the Tigers and began shooting pictures of the two men as they compared their batting grips. "Is that Ty Cobb?" I asked two women in the row behind me.

They giggled when I turned back to the field. I listened to their conversation and overheard them commenting on how handsome Ty Cobb was, especially compared with Honus Wagner.

"They call him The Flying Dutchman," one of them said to the other, "but he looks like he can barely *walk*!" They convulsed into more giggles.

I turned around again and glared at them. "Wagner's gonna run all over the Tigers today," I boasted. Without thinking, I added, "Ty Cobb sucks."

The two women looked at me as if they had seen a ghost. One of them closed her eyes and started fanning herself, like she was going to faint. They quickly gathered up their coats and hats and stormed out of their seats in a huff. I guess I told *them*.

There was a newspaper beneath my seat. A headline on the front page read . . .

WILBUR WRIGHT EXPLAINS HIS AEROPLANE.
FOR THE FIRST TIME AVIATOR COMPARES
VARIOUS TYPES OF FLYING MACHINES,
SHOWS WHEREIN HIS IS SUPERIOR
AND INDICATES REMARKABLE FLIGHTS
POSSIBLE IN THE FUTURE

I was reading the story and chuckling to myself, when I felt a hard tap on my shoulder. I turned around and a policeman was standing there holding a nightstick menacingly. The two women I had been speaking with stood behind him, smirking.

"You bothering these ladies, chum?" he asked.

"Oh, no, officer," I replied. "Just discussing the merits of the respective teams, sir."

"What's your name, buddy?"

I thought for a second.

"Wagner," I told him. "Butts Wagner."

"Honus' big brother?" The cop was suddenly acting nice to me. "I'm terribly sorry, sir. Good luck today! Enjoy the game."

He shot the women a look as he left. I smiled at them pleasantly before turning back to the field. They were whispering to each other so I couldn't hear, but I thought one of them said, *"He's* nearly as ugly as his *brother."*

I opened the newspaper again. There was no sports section, but after searching around I finally found an article about the World Series . . .

DETROIT, Oct. 14.—Detroit kept in the great fight for the world's baseball championship by defeating Pittsburg, 5 to 4, to-day in a battle full of thrilling incidents and to-night the teams are tied with three victories each. The seventh and deciding game will be played here Saturday.

I turned back to face the ladies behind me. They looked at me like I was an insect.

"Excuse me," I said in my sweetest voice, "What day is it today?"

"Saturday," they muttered through clenched teeth.

Game 7 of the 1909 World Series! And I had a box seat!

From reading the newspaper I learned that neither the Tigers nor the Pirates had won a World Series since the tradition began.

The 1909 pennant, I found out, was the Tigers' third in a row. They lost the World Series in 1907 and 1908, so Cobb and his teammates wanted desperately to win this one.

The Pirates hadn't been in the Series since they lost the first one to Boston in 1903. Honus was playing this Series as if his life depended on it, the newspaper article said. In Game 3, he reached first base five times and stole second four times. In Game 5, he was hit by a pitch and then stole second, third, and came home when the throw to third sailed into left field.

Ty Cobb and Honus Wagner had each won the batting championship in their respective leagues during the season, so the World Series was made out to be a duel between baseball's two best players. "The Antelope versus the Buffalo," was the way the newspaper described them. Honus, apparently, was the Buffalo.

Pittsburgh had won all the odd-numbered games, 1, 3, and 5. Detroit took the even-numbered ones, 2, 4, and 6. This would be the first time the World Series would be decided in its final game. There was a buzz of excitement building as the stands filled.

"Play Ball!" shouted the umpire. The big clock said three-thirty.

A guy with a huge megaphone announced the starting lineups. He walked in foul territory from the third-base side to the first-base side, shouting loudly enough for everybody in the stands to hear.

The pitcher for the Tigers was "Wild Bill" Donovan, who, according to the megaphone man, had won eight games and lost seven during the season. Bobby Byrne, Pittsburgh's third baseman, stepped up to the plate to lead off the game.

Donovan's first pitch was wide for ball one. His second pitch was high and Byrne laid off it. Ball two. Donovan's third pitch was way inside. Byrne jackknifed out of the way, but the ball smacked him on the shoulder. The crowd let out a gasp, but Byrne got up and received a polite round of applause as he jogged to first base.

I could tell why Donovan was called "Wild Bill."

Tommy Leach, the Pirate center fielder, was up next. He squared around to bunt and dropped a slow roller on the grass. Donovan jumped off the mound and pounced on the ball. He thought about throwing to second, but decided against it and fired the ball accurately to first. Byrne slid into second safely. One out.

Next up was Fred Clarke, who played left field for Pittsburgh and was also the manager of the team. Before he stepped into the batter's box, Clarke flashed a series of signals to Bobby Byrne, the runner on second. One of them must have been hit-and-run, because on the first pitch Clarke took a swing as Byrne took off for third.

The only problem was Clarke didn't connect. The catcher, Charley Schmidt, snapped a throw to third that had Byrne beat. George Moriarty, the Detroit third baseman, had the base blocked. Byrne's only chance was to knock the ball away. He slid in hard, crashing into Moriarty, feet first.

Both players were lying on the ground, but Moriarty held the ball in his hand. Two outs. Moriarty stood up gingerly, limping around the third-base bag. Tommy Byrne was down in the dirt for a long time holding his right ankle. Finally, his teammates came off the bench and carried him off the field.

They play this game rough, I thought. I wondered if Byrne would have slid in so hard and Moriarty would have stood his ground if they were each making two million dollars a season.

As play resumed, Wild Bill Donovan threw several

more pitches out of the strike zone. Fred Clarke walked to first.

"Now batting for Pittsburgh," shouted the megaphone man, "Honnnnnnnus Wagggggggner!"

12

HONUS PICKED OUT A RED BAT AND STRODE TO THE PLATE, confident but not cocky. I studied his stance carefully. He used a long bat and stood far from the plate. He held his hands four or five inches apart on the bat, with his left hand—the lower hand—about a palm-width above the handle.

He looked like he was sitting on a stool. He bent his knees slightly, leaning forward as the pitcher went into his windup, then exploded into a chopping, lunging swing, stepping into the ball.

I only got to see Honus swing once, because Donovan didn't give him anything good to hit. After ball four, Honus trotted to first base. Fred Clarke advanced to second.

The Pirates had the chance to stage a two-out rally, but Dots Miller hit an easy bouncer to short. Honus

He looked like he was sitting on a bar stool. He bent his knees slightly, leaning forward as the pitcher went into his windup, then exploded into a chopping, lunging swing . . .

slid hard into second, but it was too late. He was forced out. Despite two walks and one hit batsman, the Pirates were gone in the first without scoring a run.

Charles "Babe" Adams came out to the mound to pitch for the Pirates. Adams was a rookie, who won twelve games and lost only three during the season. I read in the paper that he was the star of the Series so far, winning the first game 4-1, and beating the Tigers in Game 5, 8-4. He went the distance in both games.

Adams was pitching on two day's rest, but it looked like he still had a jinx over the Tigers. They went down one, two, three in the first inning. Ty Cobb batted third and, to the dismay of the ladies sitting behind me, grounded out.

As Honus trotted back to the bench, I watched carefully to see if he was going to give me his secret signal. He only winked at me.

Wild Bill Donovan couldn't get loose, and he walked three more Pirates in the second inning. With the help of a stolen base, a bunt, and a sacrifice fly, Pittsburgh scratched out two runs. Wild Bill had walked six batters in two innings.

This was "inside baseball," which I've read about so much in my baseball books. Pitching, defense, running, and brains were used to win ball games, not home runs. Only a fool would swing for the fences in the dead ball era.

I noticed that the ball wasn't white anymore. There was dirt all over it and nobody seemed to mind. The spitball was legal, it occurred to me, and both pitchers might be throwing them.

The Pirates picked up two more runs in the fourth inning. Wild Bill Donovan was out of the game, but the new pitcher, "Wabash George" Mullin, wasn't much better. He walked the first batter he faced. An intentional walk to Honus and two singles gave Pittsburgh a 4-0 lead.

Meanwhile, Babe Adams had the Tigers handcuffed. His curveball was mystifying them. They could barely hit a ball out of the infield. Honus scooped up a couple of grounders, looking about as graceful as a snowplow. But he always made the play.

When Ty Cobb came up to lead off the bottom of the fifth inning, Detroit was on edge. Time was running out and the World Series was slipping away from the Tigers. The crowd was screaming for Cobb to get a rally going.

He looked like a demon at the plate. He had the weight of all Detroit on his shoulders. But like any great hitter, he was able to channel his aggression into the task at hand. Instead of swinging wildly at any pitch Adams threw, he carefully looked them over. If he didn't see one he liked, he refused to pull the trigger. Cobb finally walked.

"Wahoo Sam" Crawford was up. I remembered that his baseball card indicated he was called "Wahoo" because he came from Wahoo, Nebraska.

Ty Cobb on first base was like a bucking bronco about to be released from its pen. He danced off the base, daring and taunting Babe Adams to try and pick him off. Adams refused to throw over, which seemed to enrage Cobb. He yelled at Adams. Adams told Cobb to shut up, and a few other things I can't repeat here.

Cobb turned his attention to Honus at short. "Hey Krauthead!" he shouted loud enough so everyone in the ballpark could hear, "You better look out, 'cause I'm coming down on the next pitch!"

From his shortstop position, Honus got the message. He looked straight at Cobb, nodding his head. I could see him mouth the words, "I'll be waiting."

Adams went into his windup and Cobb bolted from first. He got a good jump and he was fast. Honus dashed over and straddled the second base bag, waiting for the throw.

The Pirate's catcher, George Gibson, handled the pitch cleanly and whipped the ball to second base on a line. The throw was there at about the same instant as Cobb's flashing spikes. Honus caught the ball, applied a slap-tag on Cobb's face, and tumbled on top of him.

Cobb bolted from first. Honus dashed over and straddled the second base bag. The throw was there at about the same instant as Cobb's flashing spikes.

The ump jerked his thumb up. "Yer *ouuuuttt!*" he boomed.

When Cobb got up off the ground, there was blood all over his mouth and chin. The Detroit fans booed lustily. Honus looked at his hand as he got up and returned to his position, like it was just another play.

The benches didn't empty. There was no fight. Cobb wiped the blood from his mouth with his sleeve. Before jogging back to the bench, he tossed Honus a look. It wasn't a look of anger, it was a look of respect.

After that, the Tigers went down weakly in the fifth. It was still 4-0.

As Honus trotted in from his shortstop position at the end of the inning, he looked straight at me and patted his right shoulder with his left hand.

The signal!

I quickly got out of my seat and made my way to the tunnel behind the Pittsburgh bench.

"Quick!" Honus said when he saw me. "Take off your clothes and put on mine." He began stripping off his uniform as if it was on fire.

"Why?!" I asked. "What's going on?"

"I caught one of Cobb's spikes while I was tagging him," Honus explained, showing me a deep gash on his hand. "I'm due up this inning and I can't hold a bat."

"So what do you want *me* to do?"

Honus put his good hand on my shoulder and looked me in the eye. "Stosh," he said, "I need you to be my—my designated hitter."

"You gotta be kidding!"

"Hurry up!" He began ripping my clothes off and putting them on himself.

I couldn't stand there in the tunnel in my underwear. I put his uniform on.

"You're out of your mind!" I said as I slipped on the thick felt pads he wore under his socks to absorb the impact of slashing spikes. "You're crazy, Honus!"

"It's a simple game," he said, helping me on with the uniform shirt. "You catch the ball and throw it where it's supposed to go. You hit the ball and run like hell. There ain't much to bein' a ballplayer, if you're a ballplayer. And you're a ballplayer. Now it's time for you to prove it to yourself."

I began to protest, but he grabbed my head with both his massive hands and locked eyes with me. "Didn't you say your dream was to play in a big-league game? Well, your dream is about to come true."

"I can't—"

"Stosh! What's the secret to bein' a great ball-player?" he demanded.

"The secret to being a great ballplayer," I remembered, "is to trick yourself into thinking you already are one."

"Right!" Honus proclaimed. "And you *are* one. You're Honus Wagner! Now go make me proud of you."

Honus gave me a shove up the ramp toward the bench. "You're scheduled to bat fourth this inning," he said, as I put my hand on the doorknob. "So if anybody gets onto base, you'll get your ups. Now go get 'em! And meet me back here afterwards. I gotta go wash this hand before it gets infected."

"Aren't you going to give me any advice or anything?" I asked. "A batting tip?"

"Yeah," Honus said. "If you hit the ball in the middle of the field, two guys chase it. But if you hit it down the lines, only one chases it. So hit it down the lines."

"*That's* your advice?!"

"Just slam any that looks good, Stosh."

The door opened right into the back of the Pittsburgh bench. I slid onto the bench as casually as possible and pulled the cap down low over my eyes so nobody would notice my face. My heart was racing.

The inning was already underway. There was one out. Wabash George Mullin was still on the mound for the Tigers. I prayed that he'd retire the Pirates one, two, three, so I wouldn't have to hit. But Tommy Leach slammed a double to left.

If Fred Clarke could somehow hit into a double play, I figured, the inning would be over and my major league career with it.

But Clarke walked. Now there were runners at first and second.

"Now batting for Pittsburgh," the megaphone man boomed, "Honnnnnnnus Waggggggggggner!"

My heart was pounding like a jackhammer. I could have simply opened that door again and ran out of there. Honus would just have to deal with the situation.

But something inside made me get off the bench and walk onto the field. This was my dream, I thought to myself. Make the most of it. I pulled the Pittsburgh cap down as far as I could without blocking my vision. I kneeled down to pick up Honus's red bat and headed for the plate.

There were a few jeers from the Detroit crowd, but I could barely hear them. I focused on what Honus had told me: "The secret to bein' a great ballplayer is to trick yourself into thinkin' you already are one."

I stepped into the rear of the batter's box, just like Honus did. I gripped the bat the way he did too, with my hands apart. Mullin looked in for the sign.

Cobb was playing right field, but that didn't stop him from making his presence known. He cupped his hands over his mouth and shouted, "Hey! Elephant

ears! You should join the circus, you dumb
Dutchman!"

Somehow, it didn't bother me. I spat on the ground,
just to show 'em I was a big leaguer. Mullin zipped
in strike one. I looked it over.

"Krauthead!" screamed Cobb as Mullin delivered
the next pitch. "Next time I slide in, I'm gonna tear
your head off!"

Mullin caught the outside corner with a curveball,
and I was in the hole with an 0-2 count. Now I had
to protect the plate. Swing at anything close, I told
myself. Just make contact. Leach and Clarke took
short leads from first and second.

Mullin looked in for the sign, went into his windup,
threw his arms up over his head, and kicked his leg
up. I followed the motion and saw the ball in his hand
at the point of release.

He was trying to spot another curve on the outside
corner, but he missed and it was coming right over
the heart of the plate. I saw it like it was in slow
motion—the ball as fat as a cantaloupe. The spin of
the stitches. My bat meeting it in a head-on collision.
I felt a power in my wrists, arms, and shoulders that
was new to me.

With the crack of the bat, Clarke and Leach were
off, scooting around the bases. I pulled the ball good.
I knew that. It was a screamer just inside the third-
base line.

He was trying to spot another curve on the outside corner, but he missed and it was coming right over the heart of the plate. I saw it like it was in slow motion—the ball as fat as a cantaloupe.

Instinct told me to run, and my feet carried me around first base. I saw left fielder Davey Jones giving chase, so I turned on the jets and headed for second. The ball bounced off the corner of the grandstand and skittered across the outfield. Leach and Clarke had already crossed the plate.

I was rounding second just as Jones finally came up with the ball, and I figured I could beat his throw to third. I did. The throw was off line, and the ball skipped away from the third baseman. Schmidt, the catcher, was backing up third base, but the ball got past him, too.

Nobody was covering home plate, so instead of sliding into third I decided to keep on going and make a try for home. I jabbed the third-base bag with my right foot and pushed off, shifting into high gear.

Schmidt tried to run down the ball, but it was hopeless. I crossed the plate standing up.

Three runs! Pirates 7, Tigers 0. Detroit fans were booing, but again, I didn't hear them. My chest was heaving.

I yanked the cap down low over my face after I crossed the plate. I put my hands up for high fives, but nobody high-fived me. Instead, the other Pirates pounded me all over. I made some grateful grunts and found myself an isolated spot at the end of the bench.

When things calmed down and it seemed like no-body was looking, I opened the door and snuck back into the tunnel beneath the ballpark.

Honus was waiting for me, with a bandage on his hand. "I *knew* you could do it!" he shouted, throwing his arms around me in a bone-crushing bear hug. "Now quick, let's swap clothes again. We're up 7-0 now, so I can go back in and fake it the rest of the game.

"You mean I can't take your place at shortstop?" I said, smiling.

"*Nobody* can take my place at short," Honus said, laughing. "I'll meet you in the clubhouse after the game. Now it's time for *my* dream to come true."

13

WITH A SEVEN-RUN LEAD, THE GAME WAS OUT OF REACH for the Tigers. Bennett Park was like a tomb. "Let the bat boy pitch!" somebody hooted.

I watched the rest of the game from my seat. Adams shut down Detroit over the last three innings and the Pirates won 8-0. The World Championship, for the first time, belonged to Pittsburgh. Ty Cobb went 0 for 4. At the end of the game he kicked a bat halfway to the bench.

After Adams recorded the final out, I made my way down to the Pirate clubhouse. *Madhouse* was more like it. The players were screaming their heads off.

"Hip hip hooray!" they chanted, lifting Babe Adams on their shoulders. Adams had won his third game of the Series, and he looked like a kid who just tasted ice cream for the first time.

PIRATES TRIUMPH; WORLD'S CHAMPIONS

Pittsburg's Great Team Wins Final Game from Detroit by Score of 8 to 0.

YOUNG ADAMS IS A HERO

New Member of Pitching Staff Leads His Fellows to Victory in Three of the Four Games Won by Victors.

DETROIT, Oct. 16.—Pittsburg won world's baseball championship at Bennett Park to-day by defeating Detroit by the overwhelming score of 8 to 0; in seventh and decisive game of one of greatest battles ever fought for world's title. This gives the National League champions the victory by count of 4 games to 3. This is the third successive defeat of the American League champions in the world's series, and consequently the third straight victory for the National League, the Chicago team having defeated Detroit in 1907 and 1908. To Charles Adams, the phenomenal young pitcher, formerly of the Louisville American Association's share of the and his wonderful Wagner, Leach, Pittsburg stars in day's victory was and he held Detroit the entire game, and in only one Detroit get more than one safety. Adam allowed only one base on balls, and four innings he retired the hard-hitter

PITTSBURG GOES BASE BALL MAD AS PIRATES WIN

STREET CAR TRAFFIC STOPPED WHILE FANS CELEBRATE VICTORY.

PICTURES OF "BABE" ADAMS CARRIED IN PARADES OF ENTHUSIASTS.

City Plans Royal Welcome for Homecoming of Clarke's World's Champion Base Ball Team.

PITTSBURG, Oct. 16.—Pandemonium reigns here to-night. Fans have been turned over to the base ball enthusiasts, who are wild in celebrating and victory of the Pittsburg Base Ball club today and the winning of the world's championship.

"BABE" ADAMS TAKES HIS THIRD CONTEST OF SERIES, HOLDING DETROIT SCORELESS

Jennings' Crew Unable to Get to Fred Clarke's Star Youngster From Louisville.

TOO COLD FOR BILL DONOVAN

Great Veteran Allows Six Passes and Hits One in Two Innings; Mullin Was Hit Hard.

By H. G. SALSINGER.
Charles "Babe" Adams yesterday afternoon defeated the Tigers for the third time, winning the seventh and deciding game of the world's championship series of 1909 and shutting out Hughie Jennings' men, 8 to 0. It is the third successive world's series Detroit has lost.

One man, Adams, won the highest honors in base ball for Pittsburg

RECORDS ESTABLISHED IN ATTENDANCE AND RECEIPTS FOR WORLD SERIES OF 1909

WINNING PLAYERS GET $1,745.65 EACH; LOSERS DRAW DOWN $1,539.99; EACH CLUB MAKES $51,272.57; TOTAL ATTENDANCE, 145,444.

OUTCOME DOES NOT PROVE PITTSBURG IS BETTER THAN TIGERS

Clarke's Generalship and Pitching of Adams Gave Pirates the World's Championship.

HANS WAGNER THE BIG STAR

Detroit Weakest in Catching Department; National Leaguers Ran Wild on Bases While Gibson Held the Tigers.

By W. W. NAUGHTON.
No regrets are to be offered on the part of yesterday as it stands a postmortem on the one but the game there is little to

Pittsburg had the pitching, Detroit did not.

Clarke saved Adams for the final struggle and the event played to him surely of the event played to him and the American league diamonds and holding them at his mercy whenever time innings of play.

THERE WERE WILD CHEERS BY CROWD FROM PITTSBURG

FANDOM IN MOURNING WHEN PIRATES WIN WORLD'S CHAMPIONSHIP.

ALL VISITORS TAUNT DEFEATED CITY AND JEERS MEN OF JENNINGS.

By LEE ANDERSON.

Adams shut the Tigers down over the last three innings and the Pirates won the game 8-0. The World Championship, for the first time, belonged to Pittsburgh.

After Adams tumbled to the floor, they went after Honus.

"A toast to the man who outhit and outran the mighty Cobb!" manager Fred Clarke shouted above the noise. "Hip hip hooray!" They all chanted and paraded Honus around the clubhouse on their shoulders.

Honus spotted me as they were letting him down. He came over and threw his arms around me. "We couldn't have done it without you," he shouted in my ear. "I hope you believe me now. You got the tools to be a good player."

Both of our dreams had come true, I realized. Honus won the World Series, and I played in the majors.

"Honus, what if Cobb hadn't spiked your hand?"

"Oh, I woulda found a way to get you in the game, Stosh," he said. "As soon as I saw you all grown-up, I said to myself I'm gonna get this man in a major league game one way or another."

Honus led me over to his locker, a gray, metal-wire thing that was junkier than the one I have at school. "I got somethin' for you," he said. "I know they're in here somewhere."

"You've given me enough already," I protested.

"Oh, you'll really like this."

As Honus rummaged through his bats and gloves and clothes, I looked at the pictures on the door of his locker. There was a photo of an older couple sitting in a formal living room, probably his parents. Below that was a fuzzy photo of a young woman, pretty, with long hair.

She was standing in a garden. There was a jagged rip on the left side of the photo, and the girl's hand was extended out to the side with the rip, as if she had been holding hands with somebody.

Suddenly it hit me. This was the other half of the picture Miss Young had given me when I cleaned out her attic!

"Honus!" I said urgently, "Honus!"

Honus pulled his head out of his locker. "Geez, kid, you're white as a ghost!" he said. "Are you okay?"

"Who's that girl in the picture?" I asked, pointing at it.

"My girlfriend," he said. "Old girlfriend, anyway."

"What happened?"

"We met when I played for Louisville," he said wistfully. "When I went to Pittsburgh, I promised her I'd come back and marry her. As we were sayin' our goodbyes, she tore this picture of us in half. She kept the half with me in it and gave me the half with her in it. We said we'd tape the picture together again when I came back to Louisville. But I never did."

"Why not, Honus?"

"Oh, I heard somebody else was courtin' 'er. Years

went by and it became harder and harder for me to go see 'er. I never saw 'er again."

Honus's eyes looked watery. "I'm thirty-five now and I haven't found anyone else who I want to spend much time with. Guess I never will."

"Honus, was her name Amanda Young?"

He looked at me, startled. "How did *you* know?"

I reached into my backpack and pulled out the picture Miss Young had given me of the Louisville ballplayer. As I held it up for him, his jaw dropped. He sat down heavily on a stool, dazed.

"Stosh, where'd you *get* that?"

"Honus," I said softly, "Amanda Young lives next door to me."

"She's still alive in *your* time?"

"She's very old," I explained. "She never married, and she still remembers you. I found your baseball card while I was cleaning out her attic."

Honus shook his head, trying to absorb what I told him.

"Hey!" I brightened. "Why don't you come back to Louisville with me, and I'll re-introduce you to her. I'm getting pretty good at this time-travel stuff."

Honus didn't say anything for a moment or two. "No, it's too late now," he said finally. "I had my chance with Mandy. Guess I'm just not very good with women. Besides, I belong in this time, Stosh.

I've gotta defend our World Series title next season, right?"

There was a hubub at the other end of the locker room. "Winner's shares!" announced Fred Clarke. "Anybody want their check?" Clarke stood on a bench calling each player's name and handing out envelopes.

"Adams . . . Leach . . . Byrne . . . Wagner . . ."

While Honus went to get his check, I looked closely at the picture of Amanda Young. She was really beautiful. It was so sad that she and Honus never got together again.

That gave me an idea. Carefully, I took the photo off the door of the locker and put it in my backpack.

Honus came over and showed me his check. It was for $1,745.65. "Earned every penny of this," he said proudly.

"What are you going to do with the money?" I asked.

"There's a home for boys in Pittsburgh," he said. "When I have some extra cash, I usually give it to them."

"You're going to *give away* your winner's share?" I couldn't believe it. "You could probably buy a house with that money."

"I got a roof over my head," he said. "The boys

need it more than me. I know what it's like to be poor."

"But Honus, why? How can you be so unselfish?"

"Hey, I'm as selfish as the next guy," Honus snapped. "You think I don't get anything out of this?"

"What do you get out of it?"

"I'll tell you." He leaned over and whispered in my ear, "It feels *so* good when I do somethin' nice for somebody, it oughta be against the law."

He thought about that for a moment, then laughed. "Oh, that reminds me . . ."

He bent down and rooted around at the bottom of his locker again. Finally, he found what he was looking for.

"These might come in handy when you get back," he said. In his hand was a bunch of cards—brandnew Honus Wagner T-206 cards.

My eyes bugged out.

"They gave 'em to me down at the factory when I told 'em to stop printin' 'em," he said.

I counted the cards in his hand. There were 12. In my head I quickly did the calculation—twelve cards, $500,000 each. I was staring at close to six million dollars.

"Hey!" Honus shouted to his teammates, who were still celebrating, "These'll be worth millions one day! Eat your hearts out, you bums!"

There were snorts and guffaws all around as towels

and underwear came flying at Honus from all directions.

"Lemme *see* those!" Fred Clarke snatched the cards out of Honus's hand and guffawed as he looked them over. "This guy Wagner is over the hill!" Clarke announced to everyone as he gripped the stack of cards with two hands.

"Freddie, no!" Honus yelled.

It was too late. Clarke ripped the stack in half and tossed the pieces up in the air.

Everybody laughed except for me and Honus. I sat down on his stool, put my head in my hands, and started to cry.

"Stosh! I'm sorry!" Honus got down on his knees before me. "I didn't know he was gonna tear 'em up."

"I can handle being poor and I think I could handle being rich," I said without raising my head, "but going from poor to rich and then back to poor again is too much for me to take, Honus."

Honus opened my backpack and rooted around until he found my original Honus Wagner card. "At least you still have this one," he said, trying to soothe me. "Better put it in your wallet where it will be safe."

I may have lost six million dollars, I figured, but a half a million is nothing to sneeze at. I wiped the tears from my eyes.

"Honus, I think I better go back now."

"School and stuff, huh?"

"Yeah. As much as I do enjoy your company, of course."

"Stosh, before you go, I was wonderin' . . ."

"Yes?"

"Well, since you're from the future and all, I was wondering if you could tell me what's in *my* future. Like, how long will I stay in the game?"

"I did my homework on you," I said, "You retired after the 1916 season. Rheumatism in your legs. But the Pirates were so awful the next year that everybody begged you to come back. So you did."

"I'll be forty-three in 1917."

"Yeah, and you'll hit .265."

"Ugh," Honus said, spitting. "I must have called it quits for good after that."

"Yeah. But then they asked you to *manage* the team. You didn't want to, but you did anyway. They hired you on first of July and you quit on the fourth. You won just one game as a manager."

"I'd never be able to be tough enough on the guys," Honus said. "You wouldn't know what I did after baseball, would you?"

"You started a chicken farm."

"Always liked chickens," he chuckled.

"But you kept coming back to baseball," I continued. "You managed and played for a semi-pro team until you were fifty-three. Then you came back to coach the Pirates in 1933 and you did it until—"

I stopped abruptly.

"Until what?" he asked.

I didn't want to tell him anymore.

"Until I died, right?" Honus said solemnly.

"Yeah."

"When?"

"I shouldn't be telling you all this, Honus."

"Tell me, Stosh."

"In 1955. You were eighty-one."

He stood there silently staring off into space. Finally, he looked at me again. "Will I get another chance to play in the World Series?" he asked quietly.

I was about to answer, but Honus quickly put his hand to my mouth.

"No," he said. "Don't tell me. Everybody needs somethin' to shoot for."

"I'll never forget you, Honus."

"Send my love to Mandy Young, will you, Stosh? Tell her I'm sorry I never made it back to Louisville."

"I will, Honus."

"And come visit again sometime."

"I've already got my ticket," I said, holding up my Honus Wagner baseball card.

I left the clubhouse and made my way outside. There were still a lot of melancholy Tiger fans milling around Bennett Park. The team had taken a tremendous licking in Game 7 and lost its third straight World Series.

I tried to hide the grin that was plastered all over my face. Not only had I played in the majors, but I got the key hit to ice the World Series! Plus, I still had my priceless baseball card. All was good in the world.

Suddenly, as often happens at times like this, something terrible occurred to me.

How was I going to get back home?

I had traveled to 1909 because I had a 1909 baseball card. I would need a *new* card to get back to my own time, and I hadn't thought to bring one with me.

I was stuck in 1909 with nothing but the clothes on my back and a baseball card that wouldn't be worth anything for eighty years.

There was nothing to do but go back to the hotel. Honus had mentioned he had the room for another night, and that I could use it if I wanted to take a shower or something. I dodged a few buggies on Trumbull Street across from Bennett Park and trudged into the hotel to mull things over.

I kicked off Honus's shoes and lay on the bed. "The future," I thought to myself. "I gotta get to the future." I closed my eyes and tried to picture my newest baseball cards in my head. Maybe that would help get me back to the future.

It wasn't happening. There was no tingling sensation at all. I just felt like some jerk in a hotel room. It was hopeless. Tears began to well up in my eyes.

I rolled over on my side. As I was lying there sobbing, I glanced at my sneakers on the floor.

Wait a minute! The sneakers! I always kept a baseball card in each sneaker to cover the holes!

I tumbled off the bed and pounced on my sneakers like they were a loose football in the end zone.

I reached inside the left sneaker. Nothing. No card. I could poke my finger right through the hole in the bottom. Disgusted, I tossed the sneaker aside, grabbed the other one, and reached inside.

Bingo! Paydirt! I could feel a card. Thank goodness my mom is too poor to buy me new sneakers!

The player's name was Craig Grebeck, a backup infielder with the Chicago White Sox. Bats and throws right-handed. 160 pounds. Five feet eight.

My hero! My favorite player of all time! Craig Grebeck may have been a .220 hitter with 11 home runs in four seasons, but he would be my ticket home.

The card was pretty beat-up from being inside my sneaker for a few months, but this was one situation where the card's condition had nothing to do with its value.

I scampered back up on the bed and lay on my back staring at the card in my hands. Holding my backpack tightly, I closed my eyes.

As I waited for the tingling sensation to begin, I

thought about what had happened to me. Getting the hit in the World Series had been cool and all, but being a man had its disadvantages, too. My face was itchy. My whole *body* was itchy. My back was sore. And I smelled horrible. All in all, I decided, I'd rather be a boy.

I wish I was a boy again.

Hey, what if I wake up in Craig Grebeck's bedroom, I wondered? That would really rock his world. Oh, who cares? As long as I get back to the future. I'm sure Craig will understand and call my mom so she can take me home to Louisville.

Take me home to Louisville. Take me home to Louisville.

The tingling became overwhelming, and I lost consciousness.

14

"JOE! YOU'RE GOING TO BE LATE! WILL YOU GET *UP* already?

It was comforting to hear Mom's voice, and sad at the same time. I was back where I belonged.

I sat up and looked at the clock. It was my digital clock I noticed first. It was 7:23. Then I looked myself over—I was a boy again.

The Craig Grebeck card was still in my hand. I reached into my backpack for my wallet. The Honus Wagner card was right where I'd left it. Quickly, I got ready for school.

"Mom," I said as we chomped cold cereal together. "I haven't been away for a couple of days or anything like that, have I?"

"Of course not, silly," she said. "But when you went to bed last night you seemed so angry I thought you might *like* to go away for a few days."

"You haven't gone out of town or anything?"

"Well, my exciting career as an undercover nursing spy *did* take me to a hospital in Istanbul this week, yes."

"I'm serious, Mom."

"Of course I haven't been away," she said, feeling my forehead the way she always does when she thinks I have a fever. "You know, Joe, I have an apology to make."

Whoa! Grown-ups almost *never* apologize to kids. It's always *us* who mess up all the time and have to apologize.

"What for, Mom?" I asked.

"I thought it over and decided it was wrong to tell you to return your baseball card to Miss Young. I think you're old enough to make that decision yourself."

I thought about the Honus Wagner card all day at school, and my mind kept going 'round and 'round in the same circles. If I sold the card like Dad wanted me to, I'd have a ton of money and all the things I could buy with that money. But I'd feel kinda guilty. If I gave the card back to Miss Young, I'd have the satisfaction of knowing I did the right thing, but no cash. And if I simply kept the card and didn't sell it, I would feel guilty and have no money, but I'd be able to go back in time and visit Honus again.

It was impossible to concentrate on history and science with stuff like that buzzing around my brain.

During third period, Mrs. Kelly was going over long division for the hundredth time. I decided to do what my mom does when *she* has to make a tough decision. She takes a sheet of paper and draws a line down the middle. At the top of the left side she writes the word PROS and at the top of the right side she writes the word CONS.

On the left side of the page, I began jotting down all the positive things that would happen if I sold the Honus Wagner card. On the right side, all the negative things.

I was deep in thought when I heard Mrs. Kelly call my name. Everybody in class turned and looked at me. I thought about making up an answer, but that hardly ever works. Everybody would just laugh.

"I'm sorry, Mrs. Kelly," I said honestly, "I didn't hear the question."

"The question was, 'Who can tell me what Mr. Stoshack is doing?'"

Everybody laughed.

"Joseph, what are you writing there?"

"Just taking notes, Mrs. Kelly."

She came over to my desk and picked up my notebook . . .

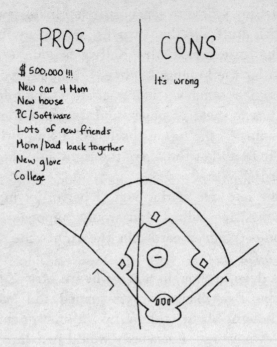

Mrs. Kelly looked the page over carefully. She was about to say something embarrassing to me, I was sure. But she never had the chance. The bell rang, and everybody jumped out of their seats for fourth period.

"Mr. Stoshack, can I see you for a minute?" Mrs. Kelly said, giving back the notebook. All the kids went *"Ooooooooh!"* as they filed out of the room.

I went over to Mrs. Kelly's desk. I was sure she was going to say something about my not paying attention in class.

"Joe, I don't know what decision you're struggling with," she said, "but it must be a tough one."

I nodded my head.

"Do me one favor," she said. "Don't make your decision by simply adding up the totals of those two columns. It would be wonderful if real life was as simple as mathematics, Joe, but unfortunately it isn't."

I thanked her and turned to walk away, but she held up one finger to indicate she had one more thing to say.

"Do you know what *I* do when I have to make a really tough decision? I think of the one person in the world whom I respect more than anybody else. Then I try to put myself in that person's shoes and I ask myself what decision *he or she* would make. Maybe that will work for you, Joe."

As I was riding my bike home from school, I made a mental list of people I admire. Abraham Lincoln . . . Thomas Edison . . . Benjamin Franklin . . . Cal Ripken, Jr. . . .

Wait a minute! There's one person I respect and admire more than anyone—Honus Wagner! And I've even *been* in his shoes!

It took about five seconds to make up my mind. I decided to give the baseball card back to Miss Young.

15

THE FRONT DOOR WAS OPEN A CRACK WHEN I GOT HOME from school. That was odd. Mom hadn't told me she would be coming home early.

"Mom?" I called. "Mom, are you home?"

No answer. The only other person who could possibly be in the house would be my dad. Maybe he came over to get something.

"Dad? Are you here? Anybody home?"

The house was silent. Mom must have forgotten to close the front door when she left for work, I figured. I grabbed a snack from the fridge and went upstairs with it before going over to Miss Young's house to return the card.

As soon as I got to the top of the stairs I had the feeling that something was wrong. When I went into my room, I shuddered. Every drawer had been opened and dumped on the floor. The closet had been emptied and all my stuff strewn around. The mattress on my bed was upside down, the sheets ripped off. The ends of the rug were turned over. My posters and pennants had even been ripped off the walls.

My mom's always telling me my room is a mess, but nothing like *this*.

Somebody had broken into the house. My room was the only one that had been disturbed. Nothing seemed to be missing. It was obvious that somebody was looking for the Honus Wagner card. I checked my backpack to make sure I still had it. I took the card out and carefully slipped it into my wallet. Then I put the wallet in my back pocket.

It occurred to me that whoever had broken into the house might still be there. I tiptoed out the back door to the yard.

Birdie Farrell was there waiting for me.

"Where's the card, Stoshack?" he said, slamming the door closed behind me. Birdie cornered me in the right angle between the house and the garage.

"I put it in a safe," I lied. "A safe deposit box at the bank."

"I think you're lying, Stoshack." I backed myself against the wall. He hovered over me menacingly.

"You're certainly an expert in that area, Birdie. Wasn't it you who tried to convince me the card was worth only ten bucks?"

"That wasn't lying," he said. "That was negotiation."

"Sounded like a lie to—"

"Shut up, Stoshack. You don't know diddly-squat about baseball cards. The value of a card comes down to two things—supply and demand. I demand it. You supply it."

"So now you want the card for *nothing,* is that it, Birdie?" I looked around to see if there was something I could grab and hit him with, but the only thing within reach was a wooden garden rake.

"That's right, Stoshack. *Give* it to me. Because it's *mine.*"

"Get outta here!" I said desperately, "You're crazy."

"I used to *own* a Honus Wagner T-206, you know, Stoshack. I had it framed on the wall in my store. That was back in the days when baseball cards were just cardboard and they weren't worth much money. Then one day I came back from lunch and the card was gone. Today it's worth a half a million bucks. You know who took it, Stoshack?"

"I have no i—"

"That's a lie, Stoshack!" Birdie shouted, pointing his finger close to my chin. "How'd you get my card?"

"You're nuts," I said, slapping his hand away from my face. "It's not your card. I found this one."

"You're lying again, Stoshack. That's stolen property, and I'm taking it back."

Birdie grabbed my right arm and spun me around,

so he could hold me from behind. He put his other hand over my mouth to prevent me from calling for help.

He had been a professional wrestler and was much bigger and stronger than me. There was no point trying to fight him.

I figured my best chance would be to get down on the grass and free my mouth so I could scream. I let him pin me so my back pocket with my wallet in it would be against the ground. Birdie straddled me on his knees, holding his left hand over my mouth while he used his right hand to search my backpack.

"Gimme the Wagner card back, Stoshack," Birdie said, panting. "Make it easy on yourself. I *know* you have it on you. If you didn't, you wouldn't be putting up a fight."

He was right about that. Not finding the card in my backpack or front pockets, Birdie expertly flipped me over. I held my hand over my back pocket, but he was too strong and pulled it away. He pulled out my wallet and found the Honus Wagner card almost immediately.

"Aha!" Birdie said joyfully. He admired the card for a moment. "I *knew* you were lying, Stoshack."

"Drop it!"

Both of us turned around to see where the voice was coming from.

About forty feet away, standing slightly above us

on the hill next to my house, was Amanda Young. I'd never seen the old lady set foot outside her house before, but there she was. In her hands was one of those old rifles I'd seen hanging on her wall, and she was pointing it at Birdie's head.

Birdie and I threw our hands over our heads. Birdie clung to the card in his right hand.

"I . . . said . . . *drop* . . . it!" Miss Young's voice sounded cracked, but firm.

I knew what Birdie was thinking. The old lady didn't exactly look like Annie Oakley. She could barely stand up by herself, much less aim a rifle. Who knew how old that gun was, or if it could still fire? Who even knew if she could load a gun?

I could tell that Birdie was weighing the risk of making a run for it. For a half a million bucks, it might be worth it.

"Young man," Miss Young said sternly. "Would you like me to *prove* to you that this gun is loaded? I have nothing to lose. I'm a *very* old lady. They could throw me in jail for *life* and it wouldn't matter. So whatever it is you're holding in your hand, I'd advise you to drop it!"

Birdie was still thinking it over.

"I heard she murdered some kid once, Birdie," I added, trying to be helpful.

Birdie let out a sigh, then opened his fingers and let the card flutter to the dirt.

"Joseph," Miss Young commanded, "Pick that up and bring it to me. I want to see what silly nonsense you two are fighting over."

I picked up the card and ran over to Miss Young. She took it in her hand and squinted to look at it, all the while struggling to keep the gun pointed at Birdie.

"Honus," she said softly.

Miss Young looked like she was lost in thought for a moment, but suddenly she snapped out of it and looked at the two of us.

"You're fighting over a stupid *baseball card?!*" she said. "Where did you get this?"

"It was stolen from my store!" Birdie shouted.

"It was *not,*" I said. "I found it in your attic when I was cleaning it out, Miss Young."

"I thought I told you to throw that stuff away." Miss Young dropped the gun on the ground and took the card in both hands, pinching it between her thumbs and first fingers.

"Wait!" Birdie and I yelled together.

Miss Young ripped the card in two. Birdie dropped to his knees, as if he'd been shot. He let out a horrifying cry. Miss Young ripped the pieces again so the card was in four pieces.

"Silly nonsense," she said. "If I tell you to throw something in the trash, then throw it in the trash!"

She handed me the four pieces of cardboard. Birdie

was weeping like a baby whose bottle had been taken away.

"What are *you* wailing about?" she asked. "*I'm* the one who loved him."

"A half a million bucks!" Birdie bawled. "You ripped up a half a million bucks! And I was so close to getting it back."

"It wasn't your card, Birdie," I said. "I *did* find it in her attic."

I wasn't so devastated when Miss Young ripped the card. I had planned to give it back to her anyway. But poor Birdie, he looked like his dog had been run over by a truck or something. I almost felt sorry for him. *Almost.*

"Joseph, help me inside," Miss Young said. "Nearly killed myself lugging this stupid gun out here."

Looking at it closely, it was obvious that Miss Young's gun couldn't fire a cork, much less a bullet.

"And you," she said, pointing at Birdie. "You should be ashamed of yourself, picking on a boy like that. Get out of here! And don't let me catch you bothering Joseph again or I'll call the cops on you."

Birdie slinked away, a beaten man. Miss Young put her wrinkled hand on my forearm to steady herself as we walked slowly to her house. I put the rifle back in the empty space over her fireplace.

"Joseph," she said gently, "what was all that about? Why are you hanging around with a man like that?"

I explained how I stumbled across the card in her attic and why it was worth so much money. I told her that I first wanted to keep it and sell it, but that I'd decided to give it back to her.

"Honus would have wanted you to have it," I explained.

"Joseph, how would *you* know what Honus would want?"

"You'd never believe me if I told you."

"I've seen it all in the last century, young man. Go ahead."

I told her everything—the power I had to travel through time, Honus coming into my room in the middle of the night, how we went back in time to 1909 together. I told her about the ladies in the stands, about Ty Cobb, and how I got the hit that crushed the Tigers in the World Series.

Miss Young whistled. "You spin quite a yarn for a young man, Joseph," she said, shaking her head. "If I told anyone a story like that they'd say I'd finally lost my marbles. Probably lock me up."

"I swear it happened," I said. "I can prove it to you."

I pulled off my backpack and unzipped it. I took out the ripped photo of the Louisville baseball player she had given me. Then I took out the other half of the photo, which I had removed from Honus's locker.

I handed the two halves of the photo to her. She

looked puzzled at first. She took the pieces and held one in each hand. Then she brought them together. They fit like two pieces of a jigsaw puzzle. The two hands that were reaching out toward the jagged edges met in the middle of the photo.

Two young lovers in a garden. Honus and Amanda.

"How did you get this?" she asked me, wide-eyed.

"Honus gave it to me."

"But Honus has been dead for years."

"I told you. I went back in time. Back to when he was alive."

She looked at me with wonder in her eyes. I was her link to the past.

Suddenly, I had a brainstorm. If I could use a baseball card to bring Honus to the future, maybe I could send Amanda back to the *past*.

"Hold my hands," I said excitedly.

I took the four pieces of the Honus Wagner card and put them between our palms. I closed my eyes and wished she could go back to 1909.

I felt that familiar tingling sensation running up and down my spine and opened my eyes to see if anything was happening.

Slowly, Miss Young began to smile, an expression I had never seen on her face. It made her look years younger.

She looked into my eyes, and I watched as the wrinkles on her face smoothed out. Her hair turned from gray to blonde. She grew a few inches, and the shape of her body became like an hourglass.

She was turning into a young woman before my eyes. A beautiful young woman, the young woman in the photo.

"Honus, I never stopped waiting," she said. And that was all she said.

She began to fade away, like a figure receding into fog. I reached out to her, but my hand went right through hers. Within a few seconds she had vanished completely. Going, going, gone, as they say in baseball.

Poof. Nothing there. It was strangely quiet.

16

"Hey Dumbo!" somebody on the Panthers yelled at me, "How about some peanuts?"

I laughed.

It was a week later, the last game of Little League season. I spit in the dirt next to the batter's box. They were hollering some really rude remarks, but I felt completely calm as I settled in the batter's box.

The pitcher went into his windup, and I saw the ball right from the moment of release. It broke in over my power zone and I belted it, ripping it up the middle and almost taking the pitcher's head off. I laughed and scooted to first.

I'd seen this pitcher before and knew he had no pickoff move. He tried to keep me close, but a right-hander has to turn his head all the way around to look at first base. Most pitchers just can't master it. I took off as soon as he kicked his leg up and slid into second without his even attempting a throw.

The pitcher pretty much ignored me. Not many guys try to steal third because the catcher has only a short throw to make, and the chance of stealing safely is small. I let a couple of pitches go by to give the pitcher the idea I wasn't thinking of stealing, and then I took off.

The catcher got off a throw, but it was a foot or two to the left of the bag. The third baseman had to reach over, catch the ball, and then bring his glove back to try and tag my foot. By the time he did that I was already slapping the dust off my pants.

Now the pitcher was really steaming. He was slamming the ball into his glove and talking to himself. I thought about swiping home, but I didn't want to humilate the guy or anything.

It didn't matter. He bounced the next pitch in front of the plate. The catcher tried his best to block it, but the ball skidded past his mitt and back to the backstop.

I took off from third. The pitcher ran to cover home plate. The catcher snatched the ball on a slide and flung it to him. I barreled in and the poor pitcher didn't have a chance. I did the best I could not to smash him up too badly. But we both tumbled in the dirt, the ball skipping down the third-base line.

Too bad Honus can't see me now, I thought, as the umpire threw his arms to his sides and hollered, "Saaaaaaafe!"

17

IT'S BEEN SIX MONTHS NOW, AND RUMORS ARE STILL FLYING around town about what happened to Amanda Young. Some people say she had a lot of money stashed away, and she was kidnapped by somebody who wanted it. Others claim she was a witch. There's a lake nearby, and the police dragged it looking for her body.

They never found anything, of course, and my lips are sealed. Amanda Young is long gone, and I don't think she's coming back.

I felt bad that Miss Young ripped up the Honus Wagner card, and I stopped collecting cards for a few months. But I got over it. Soon I was haunting the baseball-card stores again.

One day I was browsing in a place called Sport Card City, when I heard two men arguing.

"He did!" one of them said.

"He did not," said the other, just as strongly. "If he did, they would have knocked him on his butt!"

I went over to see what they were talking about. As it turned out, the discussion was about Babe Ruth and an incident that took place during the 1932 World Series. Some people say that Ruth pointed to center field and said he was going to slam the next pitch right there. Others say he never pointed. In any case, it's a fact that Ruth walloped the pitch high over the center-field fence for a home run.

The guy who owned Sport Card City joined the discussion. "Nobody will ever know for sure if Ruth called his shot," he told them. "The people who were there that day are all dead now. It's baseball's biggest mystery."

Hmmm, I wondered.

"You don't happen to have a 1932 Babe Ruth card, do you?" I asked the owner.

He looked around the display case for a minute or two, then pulled out a card and showed it to me.

"Can I hold it?" I asked.

He handed it to me, and suddenly I felt a powerful tingling sensation all over my body.

TO THE READER

THIS BOOK IS A COMBINATION OF FACT AND FANTASY, AND it's only fair to tell you which is which. Honus Wagner was a real person of course, and many baseball historians rate him the greatest all-around player in history.

"He was the best I ever saw," umpire Bill Klem once said, "and I saw 'em all." John McGraw said, "He was the nearest thing to a perfect player." Even Ty Cobb said Honus was "the greatest ballplayer that ever lived."

Nearly all the information in this book is correct. The statistics, names, streets, years, and historical information are accurate, to the best of my knowledge. The Pontchartrain Hotel was *not* across the street from Bennett Park in Detroit as described. It was about sixteen blocks away.

The stories Honus Wagner tells Stosh are stories he actually regaled rookies and sportswriters with when he was a coach for the Pirates. Honus's manager, Fred Clarke, really did invent flip-up sunglasses. The story about Pete Browning and the first manufactured baseball bat in Louisville is true.

Ty Cobb really *did* scream out, "Look out, Krauthead, I'm coming down on the next pitch!" At least according to baseball legend. And the Wagner 1909 baseball card *was* sold to Wayne Gretzky for $451,000 in 1991. So if you find a Wagner T-206 card, you're rich.

Amanda Young did not exist in real life. Honus Wagner was shy with women and didn't marry until he was 42, to a 27-year-old Pittsburgh woman named Bessie Baine Smith. Honus and Bessie dated for eight years and finally married on December 30, 1916. Eight months later Honus played his last big-league game. Honus and Bessie had two daughters, Betty and Virginia, both of whom are now deceased.

As far as I know, none of the characters in this book traveled through time. That part, I admit, was fabrication.

After 1909, Honus Wagner played eight more years in the majors, but he never reached the World Series again. Neither did Ty Cobb. Wagner was inducted into the first "graduating class" of the Baseball Hall of Fame in 1936 along with Cobb, Christy Mathewson, Walter Johnson, and Babe Ruth.

Honus's brother, Albert "Butts" Wagner, died suddenly in 1928 from apoplexy, which is a rupture or obstruction of an artery to the brain. He was 58. Bessie Wagner passed away in 1971.

Honus Wagner died on Tuesday, December 6, 1955 at his home in Carnegie, Pennsylvania, the same town in which he was born. He lived his entire life within walking distance of the ballpark in Pittsburgh.

Wagner was remembered as a modest, kind, and funny man who cared little for money and a lot for the game of baseball. It was not unusual to find him out on the sandlots of Pittsburgh after games, playing ball with a bunch of kids.

His obituary in *The New York Times* read, "Honus was such a delightful storyteller that it generally was difficult to determine where fact and fiction parted company."

HONUS WAGNER'S
BASEBALL TIPS FOR KIDS

from *Sporting News,* December 6, 1950

START PLAYING BASEBALL AS EARLY AS YOU CAN. THE MORE experience you receive, the better it will be when you're fully developed physically. The position you play doesn't matter. Just practice all of them.

I say practice all positions because a boy doesn't know where he can best fit in. Simply because you admire a certain pitcher or outfielder or infielder is no reason why you should try to play that particular position.

When you reach 18, you should begin concentrating on one position. But be sure you like it best and play it better than the others. Always seek the advice of older players and the manager and coaches. Above all, don't be discouraged at their criticisms. Keep trying. Don't be afraid to make an error. Go after every ball within reach. Soon you'll be making plays you once thought impossible.

Always keep your eye on the ball, whether you're at bat or in the field. Never lose it. Most young men have little success with curveball pitching because they fail to keep their eyes on the ball.

Keep posted on the number of outs, the score, how many men are on base and what bases are occupied. Often a player throws to the wrong base or fails to realize how many men are out. If you concentrate on the game, bonehead plays should never occur.

Study the speed of each batter and this will help you play him properly. Remember to what field a batter usually hits and play him accordingly. The percentage is in your favor. Practice sliding as much as possible. And don't forget to relax when you hit the dirt.

Team play is a great asset in baseball. Always remember you're only one-ninth of the team. A hustling bunch of youngsters with teamwork can beat a group of stars without teamwork.

THE MOST VALUABLE BASEBALL CARD IN THE WORLD

WAGNER, PITTSBURG

THIS IS A LIFE-SIZE REPRODUCTION OF THE T-206 HONUS Wagner card. It was one of 522 cards in a set produced by American Tobacco Company in 1909–10. The cards in this set are sometimes referred to as "white borders."

This card is so valuable—legend has it—because Wagner was opposed to cigarette smoking and insisted the card be discontinued shortly after presses had begun to run. In 1996, a card just like this one sold for over a half a million dollars.

HONUS WAGNER'S CAREER STATISTICS

	Games	Batting Average	Slugging Average	At Bats	Hits	Doubles	Triples	Home Runs	Runs	Runs Batted In	Walks	Strikeouts	Stolen Bases	Fielding Average
LOUISVILLE 1897	61	.338	.468	237	80	17	4	2	37	39	15		19	.910
1898	151	.299	.410	588	176	29	3	10	80	105	31		27	.960
1899	147	.336	.494	571	192	43	13	7	98	113	40		37	.943
PITTSBURGH 1900	135	.381	.573	527	201	45	22	4	107	100	41		38	.953
1901	141	.353	.491	556	196	37	11	6	100	126	53		49	.923
1902	137	.329	.467	538	177	33	16	3	105	91	43		42	.957
1903	129	.355	.518	512	182	30	19	5	97	101	44		46	.938
1904	132	.349	.520	490	171	44	14	4	97	75	59		53	.932
1905	147	.363	.505	548	199	32	14	6	114	101	54		57	.936
1906	142	.339	.459	516	175	38	9	2	103	71	58		53	.940
1907	142	.350	.513	515	180	38	14	6	98	82	46		61	.941
1908	151	.354	.542	568	201	39	19	10	100	109	54		53	.943
1909	137	.339	.489	495	168	39	10	5	92	100	66		35	.940
1910	150	.320	.432	556	178	34	8	4	90	81	59	47	24	.944
1911	130	.334	.507	473	158	23	16	9	87	89	67	34	20	.944
1912	145	.324	.496	558	181	35	20	7	91	102	59	38	26	.962
1913	114	.300	.385	413	124	18	4	3	51	56	26	40	21	.962
1914	150	.252	.317	552	139	15	9	1	60	50	51	51	23	.949
1915	151	.274	.422	566	155	32	17	6	68	78	39	64	22	.957
1916	123	.287	.370	432	124	15	9	1	45	39	34	36	11	.952
1917	74	.265	.304	230	61	7	1	0	15	24	24	17	5	.981
TOTAL	2789	.327	.466	10441	3418	643	252	101	1735	1732	963	327	722	.947

◣ = LED LEAGUE

PERMISSIONS

The author would like to acknowledge the following for use of photographs and artwork:

Carnegie Library of Pittsburgh: 79, 91; Library of Congress: 35 (LCUS262-28926); National Baseball Library & Archive, Cooperstown, N.Y.: 49, 55, 57, 70, 74, 87; "Honus Wagner Baseball Card Goes to Gretsky," by Rita Reif, 3/23/91, copyright © 1991 by The New York Times Co., reprinted by permission: 30; courtesy Pittsburgh Pirates Baseball Club: 97.

Cover photograph by Dan Gutman.